TWO SKETCHES OF

DISJOINTED HAPPINESS

S

In t
retu
dat
I

SIMON KINCH is a writer, teacher, and graphic designer based in Seville. He studied double bass and composition in the UK, before going on to work in finance, then moving abroad.

TWO SKETCHES OF DISJOINTED HAPPINESS

SIMON KINCH

SALT

LONDON

PUBLISHED BY SALT PUBLISHING 2017

2 4 6 8 10 9 7 5 3 1

First published in Great Britain in 2017 by
Salt Publishing Ltd
International House, 24 Holborn Viaduct, London EC1A 2BN United Kingdom

www.saltpublishing.com

Salt Publishing Limited Reg. No. 5293401

A CIP catalogue record for this book is available from the British Library

ISBN 978 1 78463 110 9 (Paperback edition)
ISBN 978 1 78463 111 6 (Electronic edition)

Typeset in Neacademia by Salt Publishing

Printed and bound in Great Britain by Clays Ltd, St Ives plc

*For Bob Dorrill (1924–2009): your love for
Europe passed through the generations.*

TWO SKETCHES OF
DISJOINTED HAPPINESS

ONE

I CAN'T REMEMBER the whole message. I don't even think I read until the end. Somewhere in there it said:

'You've been gone so long . . . we need to talk.' Or something like that.

I'd paused for a moment, but couldn't concentrate. I could only think to throw the phone into the sea.

The cold steel of the bench was beginning to show, the paint flaking off the arms. The harbour was empty, not a boat in sight. Turning the phone on was just meant to pass a bit of time. A couple of hours to kill before the night train to Paris. I got up and headed back towards the town.

It felt like a long trudge back across the harbour's small, pebbly beach. I clung to the straps of my backpack to take some of the strain, but still the weight dug into my shoulders. The waiter of the harbour's fish restaurant watched me all the way across the beach. He should stop being so bitter, I thought. I'd only asked how much the sea bass cost. And then I'd said that fifteen euros was too much for a plate of fish when we were so close to the sea. Most people would baulk politely at that price and continue walking. But he kept on looking at me like it was my fault, and my fault alone, that the restaurant was empty. I continued walking with my head down. It began to well up inside me that it was his over-priced fish that had driven me to that moment of boredom, driven me to checking my messages, and his fault I'd got so angry and thrown my phone into the sea. But that was just as outlandish as his assumption. I kept walking.

There really isn't that much to do in Portbou. The concave harbour is enclosed by steep juts of coastline. A single path that leads away from the beach out to sea, towards the bench I'd been sat at. A mile further north and you hit the French border. A small row of restaurants line the village beach, before narrow streets criss-cross upward towards the steps to the train station. You can either make the cheap border crossing by train en route from Barcelona to Paris, or browse information points about Walter Benjamin, who apparently died here. I read each one as I walked back through the town, but still didn't have any idea who he was. None of the information points said what he'd done in his life, just that at the time of his death he'd been fleeing Nazi Germany, heading south, and faced deportation back to France. One information point even identified his hotel.

By now, I'd forgotten about the text message and the waiter, but felt a little sluggish, so thought about getting a coffee. On the deserted street leading to the station, there was a small cafe, with a handful of tables outside. A couple of old Catalan men sat at one. One man leant forward, with his weight on a walking stick. The other leant backwards, his fingers rapping the tabletop. Neither of them spoke to the other, nor drank their short black coffees that resembled treacle. I decided against getting a coffee and instead thought about getting a Coke. I continued to the end of the street, then hauled myself and my backpack up the steep steps to the train station.

I pushed a euro into a vending machine, then took my Coke to the platform. It was still nearly two hours until my train. Wearily, I took off my backpack and slumped against the platform wall. A train stood at the platform, but headed back to Barcelona. I took a swig of Coke and swilled it round my mouth.

A young couple came past me, also clad in travellers' backpacks, and boarded the waiting train. There was a big step up from the platform to the carriage, so they took off their backpacks, with the boyfriend hoisting them through the carriage doors. He struggled with them and almost fell, at which the girl laughed and giggled something in French. This closeness sickened me, sending my mind back to that text message for a moment, and I then started to feel that same welling-up inside as I had when the waiter had glared at me across the harbour.

Trying not to think about the message or the waiter, I instead refocused on what the couple in front of me were doing. It struck me that they looked a whole lot happier than I did. Maybe because they had each other. Maybe it was because they were at the start of their travels, rather than three months wearier of hostel beds and the daily cheese-and-ham lunch. Maybe they hadn't ventured down to the harbour to ask about the prices in the fish restaurant.

The couple disappeared into the carriage. I glanced at the platform departure board, which read *Barcelona Sants - 7 mins*. Behind the departure board, there was a large poster, advertising holidays amongst beaches and palm trees. Most of the Spanish was lost on me, but I did recognise a few words. I looked away from the advert and instead at the side of the train carriage. My teeth felt fuzzy from not brushing them, so I took another swig of Coke and swilled it round my mouth.

TWO

I THOUGHT ABOUT a lot in those seven minutes, sat looking at the side of the carriage. Maybe because there wasn't much to look at; maybe because I had a lot to think about. I thought about my flight back to Wisconsin from London in a week. I thought about my Schengen visa, which would expire in ten days. I thought about what might happen if I didn't get back to London, and the risk of being deported. I tried to imagine what I'd do when I got back home to Madison. Seeing my family. My internship that summer. I'd maybe call Alyson. That is, if she'd speak to me. Anyway, I didn't know her number by heart and I'd thrown the only record I had of it into the sea. I thought again about Paris and London. There wasn't any reason I was heading there, except to get back to Madison. I then thought back to the night before, to the hostel in Barcelona. After a few beers, I'd got talking to a group of Australians. I'd asked them if they were heading north as well in the morning. They'd said no, they were heading in the opposite direction. 'Chasing the sun south!' one of them had laughed. They'd asked me to come with them. I thought about how adamant I must have seemed then to be heading north, to Paris, to London, back to what I had in Madison, and how I really didn't feel that adamant any more. And how now it didn't really matter which direction I headed in at all.

And at the end of those seven minutes, I found myself standing inside the carriage, looking at the spot on the platform where I'd just been sitting. As the beeping carriage doors closed, I felt something between a tingle and a shudder.

The platform began to move away from me as the train rolled forward. A cleaner slowly shuffled along the platform, sweeping up rubbish with a dustpan and brush. Any moment now, she'd get to the spot where I had been sat. I tried to keep her in sight as the train picked up speed. I wanted to see her sweep up my Coke can, the last evidence of me being in Portbou. She'll sweep up my Coke can and it'll be like I wasn't even there, I thought. Like I'd never been to Portbou and never sat on that harbour bench. I'd wandered through the town once, declined to eat the fish, passed on the coffee and then taken a train back to where I'd come from. If I never mentioned I'd been there, there would be nobody to testify that I had.

The return train journey to Barcelona was just as slow as the one there, seemingly stopping at every village en route. The ticket conductor was the same one as on my journey to Portbou. He looked at me a little sceptically as he stamped my ticket for the second time that day.

The train was a lot emptier than on the way to Portbou. In the carriage it was only myself, the French couple and a North African family. The father of the family kept asking me if each stop was Barcelona. I replied 'no' each time. I tried to explain Barcelona was the last stop and to wait until then, but he took this the wrong way and instead began asking the French couple. I turned to watch the sunset through the window. My original plans – Paris, London, Madison – dissolved further, becoming tenuous and weightless. My head span a bit. And in that void where all those plans had once been, my thoughts instead darted between elation and distress.

THREE

I HAD THIS feeling that I should have felt like a new man, but the actual emotion itself was almost impossible to summon. Maybe it wasn't so much a feeling, but a deduction. A deduction that I should be a new man, calculated on circumstance. There was nothing to keep going with Alyson any more. My invisible string of contact to the US was now cut, resting on the seabed of the Mediterranean. I was no longer bound to that imaginary dotted line along my map from Barcelona to London.

My connection with the world around me should have been different – lighter maybe, invigorated. But in fact, everything seemed just as unremarkable as before, if not more so.

An escalator linked the platform to the station hall. The glare of the fluorescent lights made my eyes squint, while my mind tried to suppress the station's gongs and monotone announcements, as well as an incipient migraine, simultaneously. I craved a splash of water on my face, to clean my teeth, and, most of all, to drop the heavy backpack.

I hadn't considered how late it would be on arriving in Barcelona. I looked at the departures board, searching for city names I recognised, but they all appeared to be late-evening trains to local towns and villages I'd never heard of.

The station was already emptying, a different place to the swarming hub it had been earlier that day. From across the station hall, I could hear baristas whacking portafilters against

7

bins and releasing steam from espresso machines as they closed shop. Some of the staff behind the ticket desks had also begun to leave, collecting their coats and saying their goodbyes.

I wandered over whilst I still had the chance. The girl at one window was remonstrating with a young father, but I couldn't make out what they were arguing about. The father used big hand gestures, frequently pointing at his young daughter with a flat, outstretched palm, to emphasise his points.

I made my way to the other available window. A plump, old man sat behind the glass, expressionlessly looking at his screen over thick glasses, monotonously closing down computer windows. I propped my backpack against the wall and stood in front of his window. It took a moment for him to realise I was there and then another to acknowledge me.

He pushed his glasses up his nose. I shaped my mouth to say something, but then thought to check if he spoke English first. He just nodded in response.

'Are there any trains south tonight?' I asked.

'Where to?' he managed to pronounce.

'I don't know. As far as I can get.'

'Tonight, nothing. Tomorrow . . .' He began scrolling down his computer screen. 'Sevilla . . . eight thirty . . . Málaga . . . ten twenty . . . Córdoba, ten twenty . . .'

'Eight thirty, Sevilla, then.' I fished out my credit card from my satchel and thrust it under his window. 'Can I buy the supplement now?'

The plump man huffed and looked at the clock in the corner of his screen. He really wanted to get home, but I wasn't going to let him just yet. A ticket south in my hand, right there, right then, would be the only piece of impetus I'd have left, the rest having faded in between that impulsiveness on the turnaround in Portbou on the French border and the emptiness of this vacated station. I paid for the ticket, folded it around my bank card and tucked them into my shirt pocket. I thought about saying goodnight to the plump old man, but when I looked up, he was again occupied with shutting down his computer.

FOUR

SLUMPED IN A small waiting room seat, I drifted in and out of half-sleeps, neither being fully aware of what was going on around me, nor in any way recharging my weary body. My dreams were short and unremarkable. Each dream started from the chair of the waiting room (as if, at that moment, my life held no other possibilities – not even in my imagination). In one dream, I left the chair and wandered out of the station, into an unfamiliar school playground. In another that I was able to recall, the station's vending machine stocked Hershey's chocolate, the Cookies 'n' Creme bar I loved when I was a child, and I stuffed all the spare quarters and nickels I could through the coin slot.

The waiting room started to get busy at about 5am, and by 6am it was impossible to fall back to sleep. Although wide-eyed, I still didn't feel sharp, and it was only when a large gentleman in a suit sat down beside me, where my satchel had been, that I realised it was missing.

I sprang up sharply, but it was another few moments before I felt at all in touch with reality, the lifting myself out of my chair feeling like a déjà vu of every dream I'd had that night. I glanced under the legs of the man in the suit, but he ruffled his newspaper and returned an irritated look. I circled the waiting room twice and, in doing so, confirmed what I already suspected, what I already knew: my satchel had been stolen.

As I left the waiting room and crossed the station hall, the venture I'd embarked on truly seeped from dream to reality. No satchel, no wallet, no laptop, no passport. Not even a can of deodorant.

I asked at the information desk if they had a Lost and Found, but the girl just looked at me blankly. I briskly checked every bin I could find, to see if my passport or anything else had been dumped there, but each had little more than paper coffee cups and ticket stubs.

Despite getting some sleep that night and being relieved of the weight of my satchel, my backpack seemed heavier than ever. I went into the station toilets, propped the backpack up next to the basins and took the longest piss I could remember ever taking.

I washed my hands, then splashed water on my face repeatedly. I was alone in the bathroom and, holding the edges of the basin, stared at my reflection in the mirror. It caught even me by surprise, the amount of angst that then suddenly came out. In one scream from behind clenched teeth, my fist smashed into the hand drier next to me. I puffed my cheeks out and ran through the situation again in my mind.

No satchel, no laptop, no wallet. I wanted to call Mom in Madison, but now had no phone either. And besides, there'd be nothing she could do.

It suddenly occurred to me that I might have left my card in my shirt pocket. I patted my chest - it was still there, and the tickets: my money and my impetus. I looked back at myself in the mirror and sighed with relief, then drenched my face with water. I needed coffee. I left the bathroom, took twenty euros out of the cashpoint and headed straight to the station cafe.

The barista was in a far chirpier mood than me. She smiled

sweetly at me as she handed over the espresso I ordered. I tried to smile back, but felt my face wrinkle awkwardly. I thought about maybe explaining to her everything that had happened to me, so she would know why my smile had come out so awkwardly, but my head felt sluggish and I didn't know where to start. She probably didn't really care either. I took my coffee, pulled up a chair and stared into the crema of the espresso.

I looked over at the barista again and thought of Stefani. Stefani had also been a station cafe barista, but her station cafe in Bari had been small and charming, not big and commercial. As she handed me my espresso, she had asked where I was going; I said I'd just arrived. I'd thought nothing of it, until later that day, wandering into a bar near the main plaza to ask for directions, I found her sat reading and instead of going up to the waiter, I took my map over to her. I can't remember who suggested that I take a seat, but the directions were forgotten about and a coffee placed in front of me. I didn't have too much chance to speak. She told me how much she liked practising her English – with tourists, with customers, with anyone who'd give her the time. Her family owned a boathouse on a lake in Lombardy and, every summer, she spent a month or two there. The neighbours were English, she told me, and they'd often dine together outside on the warmer evenings. When we finished our coffees, we kissed on each cheek and said goodbye.

Sat in Barcelona Sants station thinking about Stefani, that same guilty feeling – that feeling I'd had sat opposite her having coffee – welled up in me. God, it felt stupid, especially now. How I'd felt so guilty about such a tiny flutter of attraction to Stefani, that I'd toyed with the idea of going to the station the next day, to take her for coffee again. It felt so stupid that that guilty feeling had made me think so much about Alyson back in the States and that by the end of that evening, after getting through a few beers, I'd made myself feel more strongly than ever about Alyson and never went back to that station cafe, never saw Stefani again.

I span one of my spare coins on the table, wondering what Stefani would be doing now. Probably working in that station in Bari. I had no idea. I glanced at the clock, collected my things and made my way to the platform.

FIVE

I SLEPT MOST of the train journey, with my backpack under my legs and bank card in my pocket. I again dreamt repetitively of that unremarkable waiting room in Barcelona and then of pursuing some unknown girl who just wouldn't pay any attention to me. I woke up just before Sevilla, my body stiff and my mind sluggish, but when I stepped out of the air-conditioned station I forgot those gripes. There was a mid-morning heat I couldn't have imagined for the end of May, visibly rippling from the sidewalks and roads. The station was on a slight hill and, from there, the city's skyline appeared as a haze.

I took a taxi to the centre. I didn't really want to chat with the driver, so stared either at my lap, or out the window. He dropped me off outside a hostel. The building looked as if it should have been some aristocratic home, but inside, it was indeed a hostel. The receptionist had her name, Clara, printed in capitals and folded into her pin. She smiled as she took my details, which was enough to convince me that here was the place, for now at least. I booked three nights, paying cash up front.

As I hauled myself up the hostel's staircase, I tried to regain that feeling of adventure I'd felt in Portbou, or recall it at least. There was nothing though. All I could feel were the hours of travel, of carrying backpacks and sitting upright. I followed the door numbers until I found my room. I didn't really feel like socialising with anyone. Maybe it would have lightened my mood, but I didn't have the energy. There were two Scottish guys in my dorm, who really made an effort with me and insisted I came out with them that night. I said that maybe I'd join them, but fell asleep on the bed as soon as they left.

I woke up mid-afternoon, not knowing where I was. My head ached, but my muscles felt looser for sleeping on a mattress. I fumbled around for my phone and then remembered flinging it into the sea from Portbou harbour. And I then tried really hard not to think about Alyson, but as soon as I'd remembered her it was impossible not to. I sat up, pulled off my shoes and lay down again.

I thought about my room in Madison. The single bed under the window, the desk, the bookshelf. There too, just a few months ago, I would pull off my shoes and lie on my back. Sometimes I'd just lie back and chuck a baseball up in the air. I got so good I didn't have to watch the baseball back into my hand. Instead, I could spend an afternoon just watching birds land on the branches of the tree outside our house, chucking that baseball up and catching it. I closed my eyes, hoping to recall that image, but could remember neither the shape of the tree, nor the branches.

Without realising, I must have slipped back to sleep, and it was 11pm when I woke up again. Bleary-eyed, I went down to the hostel bar. I really wanted a coffee, but the bartender said he'd have to turn on the machine, so I said a beer would be fine. I took a guide to Andalusia off the bookshelf and sat down. I was alone, until half an hour later, a girl came downstairs, ordered a sangria, then came over and asked if she could sit with me. I said okay and put the book on my lap. She asked how I was and I said I'd been asleep. She laughed and said she had too. Then she told me all about her coach trip from Madrid and everything that had happened in every bar there last night. As she talked, she kept adjusting a large headband, which spread her blonde, wavy hair backwards and out. She was petite, but I noticed her shoulders seemed a little broad for a girl of her size. I tried not to think about this and instead tune in again to why she'd missed the first bus to Sevilla and why she had been asleep all day.

She asked how long I was staying. I didn't really know. I said three days. I finished my beer and ordered us another drink each. As I pulled out my cash, she noticed I didn't have a wallet – or anything else – in my pockets. I told her about my bag being stolen in Barcelona. She suddenly seemed really sorry and said that she couldn't imagine anything more troublesome happening. It kind of made me feel a bit better, even if the stolen bag hadn't been on my mind that much that day. The nice thing was that if she was that supportive about a missing bag, I imagined she'd be the type of person who'd be really supportive about all the things actually troubling me, the things I was really trying hard not to think about. And just that reassurance was enough to make me stop thinking about them.

After our beer and sangria, she wanted to go out. There was this really cool bar she'd seen earlier that day, where the people spilled out onto the street clutching mojitos. I agreed to go with her. On the way, she told me her name was Jess and asked mine. She laughed because she didn't think Granville was a very cool name. I said Jess wasn't a very cool name, but she said it was cooler than Granville. I then asked if she was from Scotland and she said no, Newcastle.

I said the accents sound the same. She told me that they didn't.

We left the main streets of Sevilla and entered a maze of side-streets, each building a different design, no street perpendicular to the next. Jess was right about how cool the bar was. It was tiny though – longer than it was wide and almost higher than it was long. Bulbs hung down from the ceiling, picking out the hundreds of copper coins glued to the bare brickwork, shining down on tables made from antique sewing machines, every chair taken.

We squeezed through to the bar. I ordered another beer. Jess asked for a mojito and we perched at the bar whilst the bartender chopped and muddled the lime, sugar, mint and rum.

She talked about how much she wanted to learn and improve her Spanish. She showed me how well she could roll her R's. The bartender flashed her a look that was neither impressed nor interested. Jess continued unawares. She stopped after a while and asked if it was interesting and I said yes. I then said that I'd probably have to learn Spanish too. When she asked why, I said I was going to live here. I was almost caught by surprise hearing myself say it. I'd been trying not to really think about that type of thing, but it just came out. She seemed a little confused at first, but quickly became very excited. She asked why, how, for how long, but I couldn't answer any of her questions. I guessed it was because I didn't want to turn back again, that I didn't want to get to Paris or London, but I didn't mention that. She moved on to saying how fantastic life here would be and kept talking and talking. I smiled at first, but the more she spoke about how exciting it was, the less enthusiastic I felt.

I thought about whether I'd be excited for her in the same situation.

It was all a little overwhelming thinking ahead too much, seeing as I hadn't really confirmed with myself what was happening. I asked if she had a cigarette, but she didn't smoke, and from there managed to keep the conversation away from the matter for the rest of the night. She got through another mojito, I got through another two beers. We walked back to the hostel, chatting about nothing in particular.

SIX

I STAYED IN the hostel for the other two nights I'd paid for. I couldn't sleep that well with all the noise and asked the receptionist if she knew anywhere with private rooms. She gave me the number of a guesthouse across the river.

The morning I left, I went and found Jess. All I said was goodbye and gave her the name of the guesthouse, should she be in town any longer and want to hang out. She told me she was leaving for Málaga the next day, but would be going out drinking and maybe to a club with a few of the guys from the hostel. She asked if I wanted to come too, but I said I had quite a lot to sort out.

The room at the guesthouse consisted of a single bed, a small desk and chair, a wardrobe and a small white sink in the corner. The building was nearly empty and the vacancies sign looked as if it were always up.

I hung my clothes in the wardrobe, placed my few possessions on the desk and tucked my backpack under the bed. I knew I couldn't stay here for ever. The rent was almost twice the hostel bed and the shower blasted only either boiling hot or freezing cold water. But for now, for a few days at least, I'd treat myself to feeling at home here.

I spent the afternoon wandering around the neighbourhood, Triana. I bought an English-Spanish dictionary from a sidewalk bookseller on the main bridge, then sat in a cafe flicking through it, trying to pick up a bit of the language and constructing longer sentences in my notepad.

In the city centre, tourists bustled along the main avenue and swarmed around the cathedral where *caballeros* peddled their horse-and-carriage rides. But in Triana, as you got away from the main bridge and the river, everyone seemed to be a Spanish local, not some photo-snapping tourist. The buildings were no longer ornate, baroque architectures, but high-rise blocks of apartments with wide balconies. Local shops served the local people. Short old ladies collected bread and groceries. The cafe patios were full of old men, who seemed to know and greet nearly half the people that walked past.

I walked back to the guesthouse. A gentleman with a caramel-coloured suitcase and large moustache stood in reception, taking a night's rent from his wallet. I smiled at the guesthouse owner. She pursed her thin lips and the edges of her mouth turned up, which I took as a smile back. The man with the caramel-coloured suitcase looked at me questioningly, then turned back to the guesthouse owner. I returned to my room and fell asleep on the bed.

SEVEN

I CONTINUED MY stay at the guesthouse. As I paid the board each day, I marked down the amount in my notebook, where I kept a rough log of what I'd spent. I wasn't at all sure on the amount in my bank account, nor the bank machine charges, nor conversion rates, nor whether to work in euros or dollars. For all the accounting, I still wouldn't know beforehand when my money would run out. Its meaninglessness made it little more than an obsessive quirk.

The only schedule I kept to was eating breakfast before they shut the guesthouse's dining room at 10am each day - a cup of filter coffee and a toasted roll with jam. I kept myself to myself, always taking the small table by the door, below a framed Cézanne print. After breakfast, the guesthouse would empty, with whichever tourists staying there either going off to explore the city, or leaving the city for good.

I began to miss the din of the hostel, of having people around me all day. A lethargy crept over me and I became timid just thinking about socialising. Tired of wandering around Triana, I spent most of my time in the guesthouse. I found a pack of cards in the lobby and would play patience in my room, or sometimes steal the daily copy of the *El País* newspaper from reception and try deciphering it with the help of my dictionary. I picked up a copy of a murder mystery novel in English from the book vendor on the bridge, but could only read a paragraph at a time before becoming uninterested in the plot.

Mornings began to repeat themselves. I thought about going back to the hostel. I didn't even have to stay there, I could just chat to people in the bar. But the thing was, I didn't mind being alone as much as that. My lethargy was stronger than any desire to meet new people.

I'd make myself take a walk each day though, always around mid-afternoon, when the spring sun beat down the hardest. Most days I was happy just to stop and watch people: outside the metro station, by the cathedral, across the bridge. I picked a favourite spot, a small cafe looking out across the river. Every day, I'd order the same, until the point where the waitress knew my order. She would see me, nod and, moments later, bring over a glass of half espresso and half steamed milk.

The Triana side of the river was dotted with small jetties – a few steps down and then a ledge jutting out into the river. Scrawny-looking kids would cast make-do fishing lines off them, while groups of teenage boys and girls sat in groups, smoking, with their feet hanging over the edge. For a few days I watched from the small cafe, as people came and went from the jetties, until on a quieter day, I plucked up the courage to go and sit on one myself.

I crossed the river and made my way down the steps of the first empty jetty, perching on the edge. A tour boat glided slowly past, the ripples spreading right across the river's width. I looked back across at the cafe I'd been sat in ten minutes before. A pair of ladies had just sat down on the table I'd been at and had begun gesturing and laughing.

I tried to count the days I'd been at the guesthouse. Six or seven. And when I thought about it, I realised I hadn't really spoken to anyone in that long. I'd been content by myself. Jess had probably been the last person I'd spoken to, when I gave her the address of where I was staying.

I suddenly felt a wash of paranoia that I'd come across too closed and irritable around her. I couldn't recall how I'd acted in her presence at all. I just wanted her to know it hadn't been her, it had been the people, the situation, but it was too late.

And when I remembered Jess, I remembered how relaxed and friendly she'd been and how she was exactly the type of person who just sitting beside would make me feel better. And despite the contently insular person I'd become, happy in my independence, if she said that we should go and grab a coffee, I'd say sure, or even a beer. I'd make the effort of going to a club with her and the guys from the hostel if she wanted to.

My mind then jumped to Alyson. And in that moment on the jetty, I couldn't picture her as any kind of ex-lover. It seemed impossible we'd ever shared a bed, shared a kiss, laughed about something together. I tried to recall something I'd said that made her smile, but instead, thought about Stefani. And then I thought about Mom and Dad and that they didn't even know where I was and that I really should call. Maybe they'd sent an email, but I really didn't feel like checking, in case they hadn't. And thinking about all that made me feel that here was the last place in the world I wanted to be. But as soon as that thought had escaped, I felt the sun on my neck, warming every fine hair along my collar, and instantly appreciated how fantastic that feeling was for the end of May.

EIGHT

I WALKED BACK from the river to the guesthouse, tipsy with this feeling that I'd stepped out from the fringes of life in Sevilla. The more I concentrated on the warmth of the sun, beating down on those fine neck hairs, the giddier I felt.

Nothing had changed around me. I still walked past countless Sevillians, nobody looking at me, nobody recognising me. I was still a stranger here. I still carried the same few possessions – my dictionary, my notebook, a pen – and wore the same jeans and T-shirt I had that morning. My pockets were still empty, save my bank card, a twenty euro bill and maybe five euros in change. I showed no more wear than the week or two I had been in Sevilla, the tops of my ears and nose caught a touch by the sun. If you had asked me for directions, I would still know that same handful of street names I had for those last few days shying away in my guesthouse room, the same few landmarks and shops for reference.

In body, I had been in Sevilla ten days. Yet some piece of me had only just arrived. Some elastic cord had been severed, releasing me with momentum. I hadn't been aware of it before, but it was only now that I felt as if I were in one time and one place – in my entirety. I would no longer cast my mind back to people in other countries, other continents, I promised myself. As I walked, I stretched my forearms out in front of me, to really feel the sunshine heat my pale skin. This sun, and these coins in my pocket, I thought. Nothing more, nothing less.

I got back to the guesthouse and went up to my room. I quickly changed my T-shirt, then splashed my face with water. Looking up, I caught my reflection in the mirror and looked deep into the whites of the eyes. They seemed, I don't know, fresher, or refreshed maybe. But I had no point of comparison from beforehand. I could not be sure if I'd had my recent perceptiveness clouded by those suffocating thoughts – thinking so much of the harbour bench in Portbou, the rail station in Bari, even at times thinking of the walk between Alyson's house in West Madison and the bus stop at the end of her street.

I made my way out into the streets again, with my now usual collection of possessions. That elastic, that constraint, had been severed – I walked with the spring of that momentum in my step. Where had this come from? Deep in my own thoughts, I hadn't considered my insularity over the past days. But suddenly aware of this, I was happy to settle on that I had either gained a freshness, or gained a perceptiveness, and neither was such a bad thing.

It was nearly five o'clock. People had begun leaving their homes after their siestas and were heading to work or out on errands. I strolled among them, through the busyness of Triana, on a back street parallel to the river lined with ornate apartments and parked cars. A girl stood in the street below a balcony, calling up to a guy in the apartment above. As I passed, he emerged, a little dazed, then mumbled something and gestured that he was coming down. I continued walking, hearing the distant sound of him exiting his building as I turned the corner at the end of the street.

The street walls and lampposts of Sevilla form a sort of

concrete newspaper for the city's classified ads. Every bus stop, abandoned shop or square of brickwork is plastered in adverts: rooms for rent, decorators and plumbers, courses and classes. In Madison, these are confined to the small windows of local shops, or the classified pages of the actual newspapers. But here, phone numbers wallpaper the city, rows of telephone numbers on tabs ready to be torn off and pocketed.

A stretch of unused wall spanned the gap between a small bar with square wooden tables and a gourmet *jamonería*, with red-trimmed windows lined with cured legs of ham. Adverts had been stuck over adverts – the paper must have run three layers deep. Jorge, a painter and decorator, had had all his telephone numbers ripped off and taken, whoever he was. Among the typed, formatted and printed sheets, one advert caught my eye. A small handwritten card, maybe half the size of a postcard, blue fountain pen on cream paper. I took it down from the wall and sat down at one of the bar's square tables. The waitress came out, with her notepad ready. I asked for a beer. She snapped the notepad shut and disappeared inside. She returned with the beer balanced on a round tray and placed it on my table.

The card was a correspondence slip of sorts. Printed at the base read 'Señora Rosales', then a phone number and an address on Avenida de la Buhaira. In the space above she'd written:

Wanted:
Native English Speaker. Few hours a week.
Holiday Apartments Business.

I took a large swig of the beer, wondering how many more

of these adverts she'd put up. It couldn't have been many. Not as many as Jorge, the painter, I imagined.

I finished the beer, paid and decided to walk to Avenida de la Buhaira. I hadn't felt it before, but with the advert in my hand, I'd acquired a slight craving to work. Such a job would be one I could do, and give me a bit of cash for the time being.

Avenida de la Buhaira was deep in suburban Sevilla. Mothers walked with pushchairs and toddlers beside them. An occasional man in a suit would appear from one plush foyer, cross the road and disappear into another. I'd only wandered over here to gauge if the business was legitimate, by seeing if the area was respectable enough: it was beyond even that.

In a phone box, I dialled the number at the bottom of Señora Rosales' correspondence card. The phone rang and a woman answered in Spanish. I should have expected that, but it threw me a little.

'Oh, hello . . . You . . . I have your advert for an English speaker . . .'

There was a pause, then 'Sí, sí . . . yes . . .'

I didn't know if I was to speak. 'Well, my name's Granville, I'm from the US. I've . . .'

'Ah, okay, okay . . .' I felt like her attention wasn't with the phone call. I could hear papers rustling, then the stamp of someone trying to slip on a tight shoe with one hand. I took her hesitation as a cue to speak.

'I . . .'

'Listen, Granville . . .' she said. There was a pause. I could hear another stamp. 'At the moment, I am a little . . . occupied . . . I mean . . . busy. Very busy. Listen – you know Café Charlotte? It is on Avenida de la Buhaira . . .'

I didn't say anything. For a moment, I worried that maybe

she knew I was here, on her street. I nervously glanced out of the phone box. But I could hear her continue going about whatever she was doing on the other end of the line. In the distance, I thought I saw the cafe she meant.

'Umm, yes . . .' I replied.

'See you there, tomorrow, at 10am. We can talk. I'll buy you coffee.' And with that, she put the phone down. I heard my change fall through the machine and checked the drawer at the bottom for any coins. There was nothing.

NINE

MAYBE, IF THE sun hadn't shone on the fine hairs of my neck, so strongly for a May afternoon, that would have been it and I would have left, giving up on a life in Sevilla. Who knows. If that feeling – that homesick despair of this being the last place in the world I wanted to be – had grown at all, I'd most probably have booked a flight home and started packing that evening.

There was a chance I could find something in the airline's terms and conditions to reschedule my missed flight, although probably not. I could bring up the theft of my belongings. But in reality, even that wouldn't work. I would follow my original plan, heading to London via Paris, and see a bit of both whilst still in Europe. I'd have had to pay through the nose for any new ticket anyway, so might as well make it from London.

I imagine boarding the morning train to Barcelona. 9am. I picture myself being sat in the same carriage as my journey to Sevilla, only this time facing backwards. The same girl in the buffet car, cravat tightly round her neck, like an air hostess. The stations run in reverse: Córdoba, Ciudad Real, Zaragoza.

At Barcelona Sants, I'd see the same plump ticket officer, the same man I'd delayed getting home that night a couple of weeks before. He wouldn't recognise me, but to me, the déjà vu is present in his every mannerism: the click of the mouse, the push of his glasses up his nose, the sliding of my tickets towards me without a word.

The wait for the train is the same. Whilst waiting, I would go to the same barista and order the same short coffee and then possibly sit in the same chair of the waiting room where my bag had been stolen.

I take the earliest train possible to Portbou, in order to spend some time in the harbour before my night train to Paris. The train rattles through every station on the Catalan coast. Only myself and a few passengers remain when the train arrives at Portbou. It's getting dark, but there would still be time to pull out a chair on the terrace where the old men had sat drinking that coffee that resembled treacle.

I'd take a wander round the harbour, now dark on this late spring evening. I can imagine the thick grey straps of my backpack over my shoulders, yet I find it impossible to really imagine the crushing weight of them. You can only feel tiredness, weight and fatigue in the moment. You can only feel them physically – you cannot recall or project those burdens. Small footlights light the path round to the bench I'd sat at before. Here I find a pebble about the size of my palm and hold it for a moment, before throwing it into the same area of water where I'd thrown my cellphone. The ripples spread no differently to the ripples of that sinking cell. And that rage wells up again inside me – that she could end it all so curtly. I grip the seat of the bench, so tightly it feels the iron might warp in my hand. Everything appears watery for a moment, then recedes. I'll finally speak to her in Madison, I think. Maybe things don't have to be this way.

I'd check my watch and see I should head back to wait for my train. The harbour's restaurants are decorated with fairy lights and, as I pass them, I can just about make out the waiter who scowled at me once before.

At the station, I slot a euro into the vending machine and collect a can of Coke, swilling the first sip around my mouth in place of stopping to brush my teeth.

Once the train pulls up, I take my backpack and board, taking a seat by the window. I take the handle beside my chosen seat and check if it reclines smoothly. Looking out of the window, I fix my gaze on the platform, until the train starts moving. The crevasses between the station tiles, the railings around the stairwells, the bin I've thrown my Coke can into. The final details of Spain. Cerbère station, across the French border, is just through a tunnel, a matter of minutes. The next morning, I would wake up in Paris.

TEN

I WASHED MY face at the small sink in the corner of my guesthouse room. Looking deep into my reflection, I tried to spot that freshness I'd seen the day before. I could feel something like it, I was certain, but couldn't see it behind my eyes in the same way as I had before.

My hair needed a cut. I hadn't had to meet with anyone for a fortnight. I hadn't prepared my appearance – rubbed a ball of hair wax in my palm, straightened a shirt collar, stretched the skin under my eyes with my fingertips – for anyone. There'd been no rendezvous to prepare for: everyone I'd spoken to recently had been by circumstance. The waitress with the notepad, the book vendor I'd bought my dictionary from. I hadn't even prepared my appearance for myself, for my own satisfaction or self-esteem. I took a palmful of wax, pushed it into my hair, then collected my dictionary and notebook and headed downstairs.

There were two handymen in the guesthouse lobby. One was on a ladder, fitting or refitting a light. The other was engrossed in his cellphone. The guesthouse owner stood below, pursing her thin lips, her attention with the man on the ladder. Occasionally she'd call out something in concern, probably worried about him damaging the decor. I quickly made my way through.

It was a half-hour walk to Cafe Charlotte. I arrived early, then spoke to the bartender, who brought over a *tostada* with *jamón serrano*. The cafe was busy, but not full. I had no idea what she would look like. Every time the door opened, I glanced up. Old men came in with other old men, to drink short, black coffees. Two younger men in suits came in and stood at the counter, both with their hair slicked right back, combed and straight until it reached the back of their heads, where it broke out into greasy curls.

The door opened again. This was Señora Rosales, I knew it. There was a way she held herself, a manner that spoke with the same tone and authority as her correspondence card. She stood taller than every woman in the bar and most of the men. Her olive skin creased around dark eyes; dark hair tied back, with looser strands falling either side of her face; a burgundy jumper, as tight to her figure as her pencil skirt; and a large leather handbag over one shoulder. Her identity was confirmed by her shoes: elegant high heels, shaped perfectly around her heel – so snug they could only be put on with a stamp every time she was to leave the house. She looked over, knowing it was me who had called her the day before: the only person in the cafe sat alone, my Wisconsin-fair skin unmistakable amongst a room of southern Spaniards.

She smiled at me and the skin around her eyes creased further. Shaping her hand to signal 'one moment' to me, she went to speak to the bartender. As she walked back across the cafe towards me, I caught myself: I suddenly had no idea what I was doing here, masquerading as an interviewee. This woman was wealthy, busy, and would no doubt be demanding. I was sat in a cafe as the only American, unable to speak the language of those around me, in a neighbourhood I didn't know. I had no idea what to say.

'Granville?' she confirmed. I nodded. 'Vicenta.' She offered her hand and I shook it. Vicenta Rosales. The bartender came over with her coffee. She gave him a smile, which he briefly returned. She then turned her smile back to me. I shaped my mouth a couple of times to say something, but nothing came out. There was a moment's silence between us, in which she stirred a sugar into her coffee.

Yet there was no need for me to say a thing. Maybe she saw me struggling, or maybe she was just the type of person who took control of her conversations, who owned them completely. She put her spoon down on the saucer and, as if that signalled her cue to begin, started speaking.

'Can you speak Spanish, Granville?' I shook my head. 'Well, we will continue in English then. Maybe that is better. So . . . you saw my advert – you know I would like an English speaker. My English is okay, I think. For conversation. For reading. For writing. But it's not quick and I don't have the time to respond to all the inquiries that I receive. I need someone for corrections, to send replies to the British and American tourists . . .'

I nodded. Her English seemed completely there, only a little hesitant. I couldn't understand why she needed someone else. I felt uncomfortable and this made me twist my knees to one side of my chair.

She continued. 'I need someone to work in the mornings – a few hours a week, only two or three days – would you be able to?'

I nodded. 'Sure, in the mornings.'

'Good.'

There was a pause. Señora Rosales took a sip of her coffee.

I adjusted myself on my chair. The silence got to me. 'How big is the business?' I ventured.

'I have ten apartments. All over the city. For tourists and some for business visitors. My husband died and he left me a lot. It makes me enough money.' She said this strongly, almost proudly.

'I'm sorry about your husband,' I said.

'He died at seventy-five. A few years ago. He was a lot older,' she said. Her gaze was no longer directed at me but, instead, at the saucer in front of her.

She looked back up. 'Tell me . . . tell me about you, Granville.'

There couldn't have been an easier question. But I had no idea what to say. I'd left behind any idea of who I was, how to describe myself. I stated the facts.

'Well, I'm twenty-three. I come from Madison, in Wisconsin, but I've been in Europe for three months.'

'Then why are you in Sevilla?' she asked.

'It's a beautiful city.'

'Yes, it is.' She smiled again. I had no more to add. I was from Wisconsin, and Sevilla is a beautiful city. The only two things I felt were concrete: where I was from and why I was here.

She finished her coffee.

'Can you do 10am Monday?' she asked. I nodded.

'Perfect. Monday, 10am. There's a cafe next to the office,' she added, taking out her notebook, ripping out a page and scribbling down an address. 'See you there.'

ELEVEN

THE SUN WOULD rise as the train made its final approach to Paris. It would filter through the carriage curtains, gradually bringing me to consciousness. I struggle to work out where I am initially – why my head is on my rolled-up coat, why my feet are raised, propped up by my backpack stuffed underneath. My first thought is the waiting room in Barcelona Sants, but the position I find myself in is even more uncomfortable than I had been there.

None of the passengers speak to each other as we file out of this overnight train. I truly wake up after a short coffee at a cafe just inside the station entrance. People flood off incoming trains, almost all syphoning straight down to the metro. My attention is caught by the clothes people wear. Nobody dresses quite like this in Madison. It seems bitterly cold for May. Businessmen bustle to work wearing expensive overcoats, carrying leather briefcases with black umbrellas under their arms. I think of the rush hour in Madison, people shuffling to work in faded chinos and Cotton Trader fleeces.

The day in Paris is disconnected. Things are on my mind. There are galleries and parks to visit and I dot round them, unconcerned in which order. The only thing I want to do is eat as well as I can, the most Parisian meal I can find. I think of trying *Steak tartare*, of sitting down at a small table in a quiet restaurant with a small, round glass of red wine in front of me. I walk past restaurant after restaurant, but baulk at the prices on every menu on every board. I spend hours ambling through Paris, maybe passing through other galleries and museums, maybe looking for that reasonably priced Parisian meal. Dusk would approach and I realise it is time to head to London, to make my way to the Gare du Nord. Maybe by this time, I would have seen the Eiffel Tower, maybe not, it depends on the routes I have taken that day. In the end, I don't care. The image in my mind would always be of that from a postcard and seeing it for myself would only replicate that. I look at more menus on boards outside restaurants.

I have to eat. I know I have to eat. Not because I can imagine the hunger itself, but because it is impossible to imagine such a day in Paris without eating, and all I think about all day is that *Steak tartare*. I eat only when I get to the Gare du Nord, only when I have looked at every menu I have passed. At the station, the only place open is a takeaway sandwich bar with a few chairs and tables inside. I eat a baguette, accompanied by a can of lager. It costs far more than I would like, far more than you could feasibly charge for a baguette – except only in a Parisian train station. I think back to a place I saw on Rue de Rivoli and their *Steak tartare* being only ten euros more than this.

As I chew my baguette, I would consider the date. It is May 10th. This is my mother's birthday, I realise. My parents expected me back on the 5th and I have neither called nor emailed. Now, I am probably missing a meal out at a restaurant with them and my sister, if that hasn't been completely overshadowed by my not turning up yet. I haven't even sent a card, but for this I can be forgiven: I imagined I would be home by now and would have been able to stop off at the greetings card shop the day before. Maybe my parents have tried calling me, constantly getting my answerphone. I wonder if they are worried. Maybe they've contacted Alyson, to see if she has news, and she has just coldly told them she has nothing to do with me any more.

I have no idea how I get to London and then on a plane to the US. Maybe I flash my expired visa quickly at the Eurostar checkpoint and the officer doesn't check the date. Maybe I can explain I am on my way home and the rules are bent in this type of situation. Maybe I am caught and deported, put in a cell and then escorted back to the US. It wouldn't be that, I tell myself – I haven't overrun my visa by more than a week even.

What happens in London is hazy. I have no desire to stay there too long, nor any reason. I buy a packet of cigarettes and smoke a few whilst walking around outside St. Pancras Station.

The sky is clear, but there would be a wintry cold that reddens my cheeks. Coffee here is served in corrugated paper take-away cups. Nobody sits down to drink their coffee – it is sipped through the cups' plastic lids as people march about their business.

I dip into the underground. The ticket barriers briefly catch a trailing backpack strap. Each station is the same. Only the station signs and relative positions on tube maps change. Each collection of waiting passengers seems no different from the last. A blur of white and red screeches to a halt at the platform. The red doors open, people pour out and you enter, squeezing in just inside the closing doors. The train moves, you alight at a station identical to the last.

I look around the carriage desperately for something, someone, to keep me in this city. A glimmer, a hint of something. I look at the woman opposite me. Her gaze appears to be fixed on my feet, or my knees, not out of interest, just because they are there.

I stay on the tube until it reaches the airport. Here, people's anticipation of holiday sun reacts violently with the grinding disorder of the airport, spilling out and polluting the terminal with airborne frustration. At least I feel some contentment in being unconcerned with the triviality of all these things. I stand in the queue, mulling over what to say to Alyson when I get back. But the woman in front is arguing with her partner about hand luggage. I can't think. Like it is a smoke, I begin to inhale this airborne frustration around me. I have to breathe deeply. The couple stop arguing and it passes.

Nothing happens past check-in. My backpack is on its way to the hold and I wander round duty-free, with only my notebook and the detective novel I picked up in Sevilla as hand luggage.

On the flight to Chicago, I am sat next to a French girl, on the way to the US. I don't speak to her for the whole flight. She shuffles through some visa documents, which I spy on over the top of my novel. Her name is Nicole. She is 26 and was born in Paris. It is a one-year work visa, although whenever I glance across, the company's name is always obscured by her passport on top. Why does she want to spend so long in Milwaukee? Adventure is not in the US, it is in Europe, I want to tell her. She suddenly shoots me a scowl and I return to my book.

TWELVE

I PASSED BOTH days of that weekend in the gardens of Parque María Luisa. The sun beat down on the dirt paths that divide the gardens, my every footstep kicking up a yellowy dust. I walked the exact same route both days, entering at the gate nearest the river, then proceeding across the park diagonally to a clearing with benches around a fountain. A hum of insects came from the shrubbery. Cyclists idled past, students talking about studies, fathers out with their daughters.

I sat in the clearing, doing little more than smoking. Only the day before, sat with Señora Rosales in Cafe Charlotte, speaking about her business and arranging times in even the loosest way possible, I had felt purposeful and organised. Yet after waking up in the guesthouse and taking my breakfast under the Cézanne print again, I again felt alone in the city, an individual with only himself to please.

I pulled off my shirt. The afternoon heat had caused me to sweat and this was just beginning to dampen the shoulders of my shirt. I laid out the shirt and lay back. I tried to push the paleness of my skin to the back of my mind, but felt overly conscious of my body. I lasted what must have been half an hour, before two Spanish girls came and sat at the benches and began gossiping absent-mindedly about something or other. I caught the words 'los americanos' and suddenly became very self-aware. It could have been just a coincidence, but I hurriedly put my shirt back on and gathered my things. They continued talking, unaware of my exit.

I wandered back through the city and, for no particular reason, towards the hostel. It was mid-afternoon and there wasn't a traveller in sight. I imagined some were still in bed, sleeping off their Friday nights. The others would be exploring the streets and arcades of the centre. Even the reception was un-staffed. I paused, before walking straight through to the bar.

The barman was at the sink, drying glasses with a tea towel. He turned to me as I came in. I ordered a beer and paid in small coins. I chose the table I'd had when Jess had approached me, taking the same chair, facing out towards the door. The barman returned to drying glasses. I took a few sips of the beer and waited.

After a while, a couple of guests came in, ordering sangrias. I concentrated on not making eye contact, twisting and spin-ning the beer glass in front of me to fan out the ring of water at its base. I finished the beer and got up to leave.

As I passed through the reception, I saw the receptionist, Clara, coming down the stairs carrying a pile of sheets. She recognised me immediately and, what's more, remembered my name, looking a little surprised that I was back at the hostel. She asked where I was going. I must have shrugged, or looked a little uneasy. My awkwardness caused her to laugh a little. I said I didn't have any plans. She then said she finished at 5pm and, if I didn't have any plans, I was more than welcome to get a drink with her. She put down the sheets, drew a map on a small napkin, then disappeared, taking the pile of sheets with her.

The bar on the napkin was only a block away from the hostel. It seemed far too close to warrant drawing a map. Clara may have sensed my disorientation, but it wasn't that bad. I thought about sitting and waiting in the bar, but instead wandered out onto the Alameda de Hércules and kept walking. At the bottom of the promenade there was a small tobacco kiosk. I had enough change for a packet of cigarettes and a can of Coke. I bought these, then wandered back along the other side of the Alameda, keeping out of the mid-afternoon sun. Eventually I found a concrete bench in the shade, sat down and took out a cigarette.

I stared across the tree-lined promenade. The Alameda was nearly empty at this time of day. Two youths sat on a bench about ten metres further up. Their haircuts consisted of thickly gelled quiffs, with the sides and backs closely shaved. The smell of dope wafted across the thick air, although I was too far away to be sure it came from their direction. I tried to make out the small street on the opposite side of the promenade. It looked familiar – maybe Jess and I had taken that route. I opened the can of Coke, taking a large gulp and swilling it around my mouth, before returning to the cigarette.

Not long before 5pm, I returned to the bar and took a table outside. The windows of the bar were lined with trellises, in place of shutters. A waiter came out, wrote down my order and returned promptly with a coffee. Clara arrived not long after. I stood to greet her and she kissed both cheeks, before disappearing into the shade of the bar. She had ignored any tone I'd set with the coffee, emerging instead with a whiskey and Coke in a lowball glass. I looked at the steam still coming off my coffee and then at the bubbles fizzing off the ice cubes in her glass. I then looked back at Clara, who either hadn't noticed the gulf between our choices of drink, or else didn't care.

'I've decided to stay in Sevilla, to live,' I told her. Clara took to this in a way I couldn't have imagined. In excitement, she reached over to hold my arm, exclaiming how fantastic that was. She then joked I'd do well to last the summer in such heat. I announced I'd been offered a small job with Señora Rosales' apartments business. She took out her tobacco, but I quickly offered her one of my cigarettes. She folded her pouch back up, then took one from the packet I held out.

'Let's eat a little, to celebrate,' she said. I surreptitiously felt my jeans pocket to check for any bank notes and, on feeling something crumple, agreed.

I drank the rest of my coffee, whilst Clara went into the bar. She returned with a *caña* of beer for me. Ten minutes later the bartender came out with a basket of bread, cutlery and a large terracotta dish. I divided up the cutlery and napkins. Clara tucked straight into the stew in front of us and I quickly followed. The meat of the stew fell apart in my mouth, dissolving into its velvety red wine sauce. I asked what it was.

'*Carrilladas*, this . . .' and she grabbed my cheek, almost pinching it, '. . . but of a pig.' She took another mouthful of the stew and glanced at me. I saw something in her eyes sparkle and willed mine to do the same.

We finished and smoked a couple of cigarettes each. I drank another couple of beers and then joined Clara in drinking whiskey and Coke.

THIRTEEN

I LOSE SIGHT of the French girl in the rush to leave the plane, although cannot tell if I do this intentionally or by accident. In the queue at passport control, I find myself looking straight into the back of a balding man's head. We shuffle forwards. My eyes refocus on the patch of flaking scalp, lit by the pale fluorescent light.

It is mid-afternoon by the time I arrive home. Dad's Honda is on the drive and the grass of the front yard is long and uncut. The paint on the house's panelling is more distressed than I remember, but I enjoy this detail. I would shrug my backpack off onto the grass and, feeling the weight lift from my shoulders, stand facing the house I haven't seen in months. I take deep breaths, tasting the air. This image of home is overwhelming, not due to the length of time I've been gone, but because of how close I was to rejecting this homecoming, how close I was to staying in Sevilla. I remember the moment on the jetty in Triana, the sun warming the fine hairs of my neck, the river glistening.

My mother can't disguise her surprise when I walk in. She puts down her magazine and comes over, kissing me on the cheek. I feel a deep relief to see her, yet this is curbed by the guilt of nearly staying away. I apologise for missing her birthday. She tells me not to worry and calls my father in. He welcomes me home very matter-of-factly, yet I can see the annoyance my lateness has caused him through twitches across his forehead. As an excuse, I tell them about the theft of my possessions and the struggle back across Europe. I try to recount the story with the feeling and vivacity such an ordeal would give. My parents say how terrible it must have been. My father concludes that it is good to see me home, then looks at his watch. He is to have dinner with his friend Harold. He kisses my mother, then leaves.

I take my backpack upstairs. My bed is made, yet buried under piles of ironed clothes left by my mother. I let my backpack fall to the floor, then carefully remove the folded garments. I notice two photos of Alyson stuck to the wall, but decide to leave them there. I take my baseball from the shelf and lie on my bed, among the folded clothes, throwing and catching the ball, tracing and relearning the shape of the branches outside my window.

We eat pork joints and potato salad for dinner. I watch as my mother prepares the food, creating a pile of discarded packaging on the counter. We sit down to eat. The joints are dry and chewy, having been cooked from frozen. Despite how pleased she must be to see me back, she only speaks about the recent news in Madison. A new housing development on the other side of town. An old school friend of mine that she bumped into, on the verge of graduating from law school. She then tells me that maybe I should get a job. Her friend Christyne's firm is looking for an office temp and she has offered to speak to the partner on my behalf. I find the fat on the pork joints particularly difficult to cut. All this time, we haven't spoken about Alyson. Mom hasn't asked and I haven't brought it up.

I wonder if she knows. I feel everything around me sink and the colours of the room fade. My mother is waiting for me to say something, so I nod and agree to the job.

FOURTEEN

As we'd sipped our whiskey and Cokes, some travellers from Clara's hostel had passed and persuaded us to go to a bar with live music. Clara had agreed instantaneously, only looking for my approval after everything had been agreed. Inside, I could barely move, nor hear the people we were with. After a few drinks, one of the guys started hitting on Clara, so I decided to leave and head back to the guesthouse. In the morning I wondered whether I'd done the right thing, as she hadn't really seemed that keen on the guy and it had probably been more about me feeling a little awkward.

I started to worry she may have been a little angry with me for heading off that night. I chose my walks so they avoided her work and avoided the bar-lined Alameda. I thought about leaving a note for her at the hostel, but in the end, didn't get round to it.

A week passed. I had started work with Señora Rosales. Most days, we'd meet in her office, although occasionally she'd give me the address of a cafe to meet in, if she was to hand over the keys for a nearby apartment that morning. Each day she arrived with a plastic wallet full of apartment brochures and information and often with a numbered set of apartment keys. I would work from her laptop, replying to inquiries or correcting her text. After an hour or two, she would look at her watch and say she had to get going, handing me a crisp twenty euro note each time. She would pay for our coffees and then I'd wander off to explore a little more of the city.

As we sat together about a week later, she moved the conversation on to where I was living. I told her about the guesthouse and the old lady with thin lips who ran it. She nodded, saying she knew where it was, and then thought for a moment. We were sitting out on the terrace of a cafe near the cathedral, unsheltered from the sun. I had to continuously shift on my chair, or else the sweat would collect on the backs of my knees and seat of my trousers. Señora Rosales kept an elegant, upright posture, her bare shoulders shaded by her wide-brim hat. I couldn't stay at the guesthouse for ever, she told me, and she had a place she could offer me in the short term. There was a small, unused studio on the roof of one of her tourist apartments, which she was planning to renovate, but not until the end of the summer at least. As long as I kept out of the way of the guests, it could be mine.

After our work, she took me to show me the studio. We entered through a doorway off a wide alleyway dotted with shops and bars. We climbed three storeys, to where the stairs led out onto the roof. The roof was edged by waist-height walls, covered in a bland, smooth concrete. The studio stood at the far end, a continuation protruding upwards from the building below. She rummaged around in her bag and pulled out a single key, then opened the door and gestured for me to enter. I went in, standing within a small kitchenette nestled just inside the entrance. There was only a sliver of light coming through the apartment's drawn curtains. Turning to the kitchenette's sink, I ran the cold tap, then the hot tap, before turning both off as firmly as I could. Señora Rosales looked at me, holding the same upright posture, clutching her handbag.

I asked how much rent she wanted and she thought for a moment. She proposed I could have it for free, just in exchange for the work I did. Smiling, she pressed the key into my hand and then said she needed to get going. When she'd gone, I went to the other end of the narrow apartment and drew the curtains. They revealed a large window, with a small balcony, high above the street. Next to me, there was a small table, pushed up against the wall, and a tall, simple bookcase. The bed was without a pillow and there was neither duvet nor sheets. With the studio now lit by the midday sun, I looked around properly. The walls had been hurriedly painted white. You could still make out flecks of the previous sky-blue decoration around the plug sockets. I turned and tested the key in the lock a few times and then left, heading in the direction of the guesthouse, to pay up and collect my backpack.

The guesthouse owner took my final pay and keys and marked something down in a small hardcover notebook I'd never seen her use before. She seemed neither pleased nor displeased that I was finally leaving. I put this down to something that running a guesthouse does to you.

On the way to the studio I stopped at a small shop, run by a Chinese family. The girl at the counter watched me closely as I collected a short stick of bread, a wedge of pale pre-packed cheese, a litre bottle of beer and some bed sheets. That would be that, I told myself. I'd spend the rest of the day in the apartment, making it home. Maybe buy a few things tomorrow, but for now, I would appreciate the four walls of privacy I'd gained.

FIFTEEN

A JOB IS a job, Christyne says to me. She confesses it is far from exciting, but the pay is okay. I take a seat in the foyer, as she tells me. My shirt feels stiff and uncomfortable. I look down at my cuffs. The thread through one button has started to fray, with a few strands of fabric wisping outwards. Christyne returns and introduces me to Robert, the firm's accountant. We go through to his office. Robert starts running through the role's duties. On his desk there is a picture of him and his two children, in ski uniforms, with a backdrop of snow-topped mountains. We go through to the main office. He shows me how to check invoices and where to file the paperwork. His hands have almost a yellowy pigment and I notice the prominence of his index finger tendon.

Later, I am introduced to everyone in the office. The only name I remember is Laura, a girl my age sitting on the other side of the office, who wears a white cardigan and smiles sweetly. Everybody in the office has identical phones, desks and computers. Even their ring binders are the same shade of green. It strikes me as odd that everybody would wish to have the same furniture and the same stationery as everyone else, but then I tell myself it's not for the firm to think about what everybody wants and it doesn't matter to me if I have a green ring binder or a black ring binder.

I would spend the rest of the day filing invoices. The filter coffee is bitter and tarry, but I drink four cups. It sticks to my teeth and tongue. I start to think of Alyson and where she is. I imagine that she still lives at home, that maybe she has a job in that solicitor's office on West Johnson Street that she was going to apply to. I make a plan to ring her house phone that night and announce I am back. I will deny that I ever received her message and say that my phone was stolen before that. She will say what she has to say. I am filled with such apprehension that I become nervous and am stapling invoices together with a shaking hand. Robert comes over with more invoices. He asks how I am getting on. I compose myself and say the work looks very interesting and he tells me that he's impressed with me so far. He goes on to say that a few colleagues normally go for a drink on a Friday and I am welcome to join. I accept the invitation, trying to do so convincingly.

Later, at home, I sit on my bed. I cannot bring myself to call Alyson. She would know I received that message and feel angry that I should bother her, when I should know things are over.

It begins to eat at me, that reason why she would end it. I think about those last few weeks together, before I went travelling. I remember one evening, sitting where I sit now, my arm round her, reassuring her things would continue when I returned. This memory – of her so upset, so paranoid our relationship could end – is at odds with the abrupt text message I read on the harbour bench. Something must have changed in my three months away. I continue to scan my mind for clues. There was a sushi place we ate at a week or two before I left. I try to remember her mood that evening. I can't remember her being that talkative, yet can't remember her being too closed. I remember trying to tell her about my trip, where I would go. About how I wanted to go to Lake Bled in Slovenia, with its church built on the island in the middle. I'd looked up that you could take a boat across. She had seemed interested at the time, but the more I think about it, the more I convince myself that she was putting it on. The only other things I remember with clarity are the matchstick-sized implements placed with the wasabi sauce and the snap of the wooden chopsticks as they split.

SIXTEEN

ONE MORNING EARLY the next week, I woke sharply, at what must have been 6am. The room was still dark, although I could make out the muted morning sunlight through the netted curtains. I tried to wrap up in the bed sheets and fall back to sleep, but needing to piss, got up and went to the bathroom. Coming back into the studio, I stood in my boxer shorts, considering whether to return to bed. I looked towards the window, towards the rooftops across the street. Through the mesh of the curtains, I could make out flickers of movement, silhouettes on the roof opposite. I approached the window cautiously, the figures becoming clearer as I approached the curtains.

A guy in a baggy T-shirt and harem pants staggered across the rooftop and slouched down against the far wall. His friend, clutching a Spanish guitar, followed briefly, before returning to the stairwell and calling out 'Raquí . . . Raaaaquí!' A girl emerged, clutching plastic cups and a bottle. The guy with the guitar laughed hysterically and they both swayed across the rooftop towards the far wall. The girl slumped herself next to the guy sitting down. I moved my face closer to the curtain to try and make out their faces. The last guy was now sitting cross-legged, the guitar across his body. He shaped his fingers and, in one movement, released a *rasqueado*, his fingers springing out like the pages of a flipbook comic, each striking every string independently. The guy in the baggy T-shirt smiled broadly and drunkenly. The girl had begun to speak quickly, whilst pouring the bottle between the three plastic cups. The guitarist began in earnest, his friend joining in with syncopated claps, his hands held high as he did.

Through the netted curtain, I watched them laugh and sing. The girl continued drinking, whilst the guys had slowed down, clearly drunk enough already. I worried they might see my outline, but not once did they turn towards me.

I took a seat at the table, losing sight of the drunken *flamenco*, the sound becoming muffled. The table was as I'd left it the day before. Half a bottle of red wine, the cork next to it on the table, rather than replaced. A plate scattered with the crumbs of bread crust. The detective novel I'd bought from the book vendor on the bridge, finally finished. I'd unpacked all my belongings. My clothes sat folded on the bookshelves, my few possessions arranged between them. I'd bought coffee and a single-shot Italian percolator, which rested on the hob. But these few things did nothing to fill the space of the studio, leaving it empty and impersonal. I re-corked the wine, pulled on my jeans and a T-shirt, and left the apartment without showering.

The rooftop was just beginning to catch the sun. I felt the chill of the morning in just my T-shirt, so rubbed my forearms to warm them up. I looked out over the rooftops for a moment, before heading down the staircase through the building.

The streets of the city centre were empty. There were no postmen on their rounds, no early-morning commuters catching trains. Sevilla was as quiet as Madison in the dead of night, only instead, hazily lit by the morning sun.

I reached the edge of the old town. Across the road, a cambered bridge stretched the river.

I dropped down to the path on the riverbank beneath the bridge and continued my walk. As I got further away from the main road, the sounds of passing cars faded enough for me to catch the morning birdsong from the tree-lined bank opposite. When the traffic was almost inaudible, I took a seat on a bench. The birds chattered and the water lapped against the concrete riverbanks. I heard the sound of patting, from the direction I'd just come from. I turned to see a jogger in the distance, slowly treading towards where I sat. His features became clearer as he approached. A man of about forty-five, fifty, with greying, curly hair, dressed in a running vest and shorts. Almost pristine trainers, black with orange trim.

As he passed me, he made eye contact. He acknowledged me with a quick smile, maybe the first person he'd seen this early in the morning. I looked at him blankly, only thinking that it wouldn't have hurt to smile back when he was almost out of sight.

SEVENTEEN

AFTER A FEW days working a strict 7.5 hours, I begin to stray away from my desk at any opportunity given. Between the rows of filing cabinets at the back of the office, large windows look out over the rooftops of the adjacent buildings. I often linger here, clutching paperwork and filing to my chest, watching pigeons peck at food and scrap with each other, or perch along the roofs' ledges.

Each lunch hour is stretched as far as it will go. There is an independent burrito place a street away from the office that I go to every day. It's still a fast-food joint, but I find charm in its small, square, metal tables, lined in rows. The shop owner learns my name and I learn his. He knows my order and, each day, packs an impossible amount of rice, black beans, chicken, sour cream and cilantro into a wrap. I eat in every day: the square table nearest the door, a burrito on a sheet of greaseproof paper, a can of Coke to wash the food down.

I make it a daily habit to grab a coffee from the coffee house opposite the office. Here, there is seemingly a different barista every day. I repeat my order – a long black – every visit. Nobody remembers it – that, or they deem it too rude to assume 'the usual?'

One lunchtime, Laura, the girl from the far side of the office, spots me in the queue. She smiles when we make eye contact and then more broadly after she comes over, and we begin talking. She asks me if I've come here before. The question strikes me in how mundane it is. I then begin to doubt myself and whether the mundanity is in her question or in the fact I come here every day. She points out their blueberry muffins, exclaiming how they are the best in town. I've never even noticed the display counter they sit on.

Thinking I can extend my time away from the office, I invite her to take a walk. We buy our coffees in takeaway cups and walk down the block slowly, so as not to spill them. The street is alive with the bustle of lunchtime activity, yet this is a hollow verve - office clerks clutching sandwiches, secretaries out for coffee. Laura's hair is pulled back in a loose ponytail, strands occasionally caught by the fine breeze. I imagine her with her hair untied, it falling onto her shoulders. Thinking about this as we walk, I am often caught with nothing to say, yet she instinctively fills these silences with little anecdotes, as sweet as they are trivial.

She asks me how I am enjoying my work. 'It's actually really interesting,' I tell her, as I'm afraid that the truth would both sour our conversation and make me sound uninteresting.

'That's good. The last temp didn't like it much. But he was a really boring guy. I don't think he really found much joy in anything.'

A film has started to appear on the top of my coffee. I swill the whole cup down, without really noticing any flavour. We sit for quarter of an hour on a park bench, before walking back to the office. In the elevator, she tells me I'm wearing a nice shirt. I want to say I like her cardigan, but worry she'll find this comment on her office attire as banal as I find hers.

EIGHTEEN

I WENT BACK to the book vendor on the bridge, intending to buy everything he had in English. He sat on a small chair, underneath a parasol with a makeshift stand. The enthusiasm I had arrived with waned as I flicked through a small selection of trashy novels aimed at middle-aged women who fantasised about being seduced away from their marriages. Anything in this vein I left, but took the remaining books: a slim thriller set in Stockholm, a sci-fi novel and a tattered set of essays by Walter Benjamin. I thought briefly of the criss-crossed streets of Portbou, dotted with their Walter Benjamin information points, then of the moody waiter at the fish restaurant. Abruptly, I sandwiched the Benjamin between the thriller and the sci-fi and paid the vendor a euro for each book. I then walked purposefully off, angry that I'd reminded myself of that harbour and that cold steel bench.

I bought tomatoes, sweet satsumas and chirimoyas from the Feria market. The grocer placed each fruit into a brown paper bag, with hands of the same texture: tanned, creased and rough. I took eggs from the stand next to him, then two rings of soft cooking chorizo from a butcher dressed in a white coat, as clean as a doctor's.

Returning to my studio, I placed the groceries in the kitchen, then went to the bathroom. I ran the tap, taking a cupped handful of water, and drenched my face. The water turned a slight grey as it ran from my face onto the porcelain below – the fine dust of the city, mixed with the sweat of early summer.

I cooked up half a chorizo in a pan with two fried eggs, letting the red juices run through the whites of the eggs, then ate on the corner of the table nearest the balcony. The balcony window ran from floor to ceiling. Moving the curtain aside I had a bird's-eye view of the street: the small cafe below, old ladies walking slowly, pushing trolleys of shopping. The odd cyclist weaved through the ambling pedestrians. At about 2pm, the waiter from the cafe – an older man – began to heave the tables out in the street inside. By twenty past, he'd locked up, the street already deserted, everyone at home to lunch, or to have a siesta.

The sun was at its highest and beating down stronger than it had that year. I felt the mugginess press through the open window. I stripped the sheet off my bed and, making my way out to the rooftop, stretched it out on the hot concrete. I took off my shoes and shirt, and lay out, basking in the sun.

It took only a few moments for the sweat to begin forming along my brow. Immersed in the heat, smothered by the heavy air, the sounds of the city were reduced to a quiet rumble. I raised my hand to shield my eyes. Above, a cloudless sky of such rich blue. This was the kind of sunshine and heat I'd never known in Wisconsin, never anything so oppressive. I closed my eyes and pictured the back porch of my house, the tree outside the window, the fences surrounding my yard. There I would sit cross-legged on the grass, in jeans and my Brewers sweater, looking up at the summer sky – yet a sky of grey-blue, dotted by cloud. The wind would ruffle the grass, occasionally making me shiver.

I opened my eyes again to the Sevilla sky above and let that image of home dissolve in the brightness of where I lay, a reality disconnected now. Only the most vivid of memories really retain their clarity and even this is relative; in a city of such light and lucidity, even my fondest images of Madison faded to loose notions, unanchored by any common sensation I felt in Sevilla.

I wanted to drop into a half-sleep, to let the distant sounds of the city below blend with the shapes and forms of my imagination, detaching my mind from the present. Here, I would explore a future, an invented speculation, and project myself onto it. But I was stopped from dropping off by the heat's intensity. I closed my eyes, but my skin became hyper-sensitive. As my awareness fell onto any particular patch of my bare skin, I could feel the scorching heat of the sun, I could almost feel the pigment reddening. Of course, all of this was my body's protection system, no more than an evolutionary alarm, yet there reached a point when I could no longer stand this intrusion to my meditative state. I returned inside, intending to lie out on the bed. But looking at the empty studio apartment, I felt a dull punch, the weight of boredom. For a moment, I stared at the unmade bed, focusing on the folds between the sheets' creases. I pulled on a shirt and headed to the street.

I walked down Calle Sierpes, smoking. The only shops not closed for the siesta period were the large multinational chains. After putting out my cigarette, I flicked through a rail of white shirts just outside a shop door. I stopped halfway, dejected by the repeated cut of cloth.

I continued walking. Here, the afternoon was busier. I was kept afloat on the faceless commotion of shoppers and tourists.

Outside another clothes shop, I caught an American accent. Two Virginian ladies stood admiring a rack of floral dresses. I stopped and feigned interest in the shop display to eavesdrop their conversation.

'Do you think Jane would like this?' one asked, clutching a dress. The second lady took a pair of glasses that hung from her neck on string and pushed them to her face.

'It's very pretty. She's a slender girl, is Jane. Is this the fashion with the girls at universities now, Mary?'

'I don't know. Oh, I don't know whether I should buy it or not. Do you think she'd like it?'

The first lady continued to talk, changing the subject to Jane's boyfriend. I became frustrated by the mundanity of their chatter and walked away.

Still on Calle Sierpes, I took a seat at a small cafe, adorned with glazed tiles, and lit a cigarette. A waiter in short sleeves came out, with a pen and notepad in his shirt pocket. He clapped his hands together to confirm my order and returned with a thick dark espresso.

Only one table was still shaded by the cafe's parasols and this was taken by a couple in enamoured conversation. I took a sip of my coffee and leant back in my chair. They spoke in Spanish and I could barely understand a word they said. I focused on the shape and tone of their voices. Her voice shaped a phrase in a tone I knew, implying that whatever he had just said, he should know better. I listened intently, trying to gauge more, shifting my gaze past my knee, to the floor beneath their table.

This girl had a thick, styled bob, with a fringe swept behind one ear, curling back towards her chin. From the bottom of a slender earlobe, a golden earring glinted. She sat away from her date, though aligned her body directly at him, occasionally looking him deep in the eyes, cautious yet intense. His responses were short and blasé. He was sitting too confidently, as if in little doubt of his powers of seduction. His hand reached out to touch hers. Without looking up, I sensed the goose pimples run up her arm. Her body froze, unable to react, yet craving to.

They continued to talk. She questioned him, demanding to know more about him. He continued his series of abrupt responses. She should have been put off by his arrogance, yet the more aloof he became, the more she persisted with the conversation. My stomach clenched. Something wasn't right, there was a dishonesty here, I could feel it. I glanced up at the girl and, in both that fear and lust I saw behind her features, I knew. I knew there was some other man, some guy who was infatuated with her. Not this man here, some other. A man who knew her intimately, who had one day stood in front of her and told her what he felt for her. A man who had engrossed himself in her, maybe into what they once had together. He had given her a love that wasn't enough, or just wasn't right, something that could never be this animalistic fling. I imagined the other man far off somewhere, travelling, moving from city to city, anything: attempting to widen a world that had once centred round her. And now she sat across her table from a man who couldn't give a damn about that love. He either didn't know he existed, or resolutely didn't care. The girl just looked at him and rolled her bottom lip under her teeth.

I told myself these were strangers, what they did meant nothing to me. But thinking about that unknown other – and that she could ignore such infatuation for this brute – left me desolate. My eyes watered. I stood up and fumbled around for enough change to cover my half-finished coffee. The guy looked over at me as I left, a hint of disgust at my weakness. The girl with the bob kept her eyes fixed on him and only him.

NINETEEN

I STAY LATE one evening to help Robert prepare a client's file. Robert tells me a willingness to stay late is one of the key ingredients to success in this business, but does so without sounding at all impressed I've chosen to do so. We barely talk as we work, the only sounds being the tapping of keyboards and rustling of papers.

On my way home I go to take coffee from the coffee house opposite. I consider taking one of the muffins Laura had pointed out, but decide against it.

It's the time of evening when the people finishing work mingle in the streets with those going out to the bars. I keep my gaze fixed ahead, on the pavement stretched out before me. By chance, I find myself walking at the same pace as a man ahead of me. Although our pace is the same, his stride is shorter, meaning he makes a busy shuffle to achieve the same speed as me. In the end, he makes a turn at Grant Street. I continue walking home.

Two blocks down, I see Clementine, one of Alyson's best friends, ahead of me, across the street. She is with a friend and must be twenty metres ahead, walking in the same direction as me. I cross to their side of the road, feeling there is less chance of them seeing me here. Clementine has her hair pushed up in a bun, and wears a jumper I recognise. I don't know her friend, a red-haired girl about our age.

We are halfway to my house when they take a left. When

I reach this junction, I look down the road they have taken, seeing them outside a bar. I take this detour. By the time I catch up, they have entered. I cautiously peer through the window, wondering if they are meeting Alyson. The room is empty, with just Clementine and her friend standing at the bar, looking at drinks menus. I am suddenly gripped by the fear Alyson will turn up any moment, come walking down the street and see me peering through the bar window at her friends. I walk back down the street as quickly as I can and rejoin my route home.

Mom asks me how work is going. She has cooked meatloaf and steamed vegetables. The smell fills the kitchen, the meatloaf resting in the oven while we wait for my father. I tell her work is going very well and say how I stayed to help Robert prepare some files. My father comes in and we eat. He asks the same questions and I tell him about how I stayed to help Robert prepare some files.

After dinner I flick through the cable channels and find an old Woody Allen film. Halfway through, my father comes into the room and asks if he can watch the news. I can kind of guess where the film is going, and hand him the remote. I ask him if he would like a beer, and return with two Budweisers from the fridge. After half an hour, my father is asleep in his chair, his shirt unbuttoned and the ends of his trousers beginning to rise up his calves due to the way he is sat. I switch the TV back to the Woody Allen film, but miss the end, before also falling asleep in my chair.

TWENTY

IT WAS ONLY when the gas in the studio had run out that I realised it had come from a canister. My eggs still had a translucent film across the whites, and the skin of the chorizo had yet to shrink and curl. I followed a copper pipe from the hobs, finding the empty canister in the cupboard under the sink. I put the pan of eggs and chorizo out on the roof terrace, in the hope that the scorching sun would cook them through. I cut some bread and returned to the pan, scooping up pieces of egg white when they appeared cooked.

I had nothing to do that afternoon, so lay out in the sun, reading the thriller set in Stockholm. I read a paragraph at a time, the blinding heat forcing me to close my eyes in between. In these moments, my mind would fall on how and where I could buy gas.

When the sweat began to run down my arms, I went inside. I stared at the empty gas canister, then went to run a bath of cold water. I sat staring into the gush of water from the tap, as it slowly filled the tub. The water pressure caused a kink in the flow of water, where the width and the depth of the stream swapped. The sunlight coming through the studio, via the open bathroom door, refracted though this kink, creating a vivid green and cyan. Staring into the water, I pictured Alyson naked, leant over the bathtub. For weeks, she had mentioned again and again how she fantasised about having sex in the bath. With her parents away one weekend, we went to the bathroom, running a bath of bubbles and scented oils. Such was her excitement though, she had us both stripped off even before the bath had filled, bending over the bathtub and pulling me up behind her.

I looked back at the bath of cold water and turned off the tap. I then stripped and plunged straight in, shivers running across my browned skin.

I have no idea how long I lay under the water, my eyes closed, my hair fanned out, my lips and nose just above the surface. When I opened them again, I pulled my head out of the water and sat up. Water ran down my back, and droplets from my elbows. I focused on each wall, but couldn't shake my disorientation. Everything felt foreign: the bathtub, the walls, the studio outside the bathroom door. It was the feeling of waking up for the first time in a bed that wasn't mine, searching for my bearings. I thought again of my bed below the window in Madison, then pulled the plug on the bath.

Taking a handful of cash from the bookshelf, I went to the Alameda. I could only think of seeing Clara again. The promenade was nearly empty. A few people sat outside restaurants; a man walked his dog past the columns. Crossing the Alameda, I found the bar with the hatched trellis we'd eaten at the week before. Inside, I ordered a *caña*, taking it out to a table and lighting a cigarette.

Over the afternoon, I stretched out another *caña* and a tapa of *carrilladas*. Instead of tucking in ravenously as I had before, this time I carefully poked at the meat in its broth, making it fall into its separate strands. Several times, the barman came out to see if I'd finished what was in front of me, but had to return empty-handed each time.

Shortly after 5pm, Clara passed. She was as surprised to see me as I was to see her – for all my waiting, I'd never really expected she'd walk past. The hovering barman took her order and she joined me.

She began by complaining about the heat and then her shift. I analysed every hand gesture, every facial expression as she spoke. All I could think about was that I'd left that club too hastily the other night and she would still be resentful because of this, but there was nothing in her body language to say she was. She instead seemed to pick up exactly where we'd left off, eating these same *carrilladas* at this very table. Eventually, I accepted it hadn't been a big deal to her at all. I asked if I could buy her a whiskey and Coke and she said yes.

I returned with two lowball glasses. 'How perfect that you were out in this street, Granville,' she smiled cheekily. She span the ice round in her glass with the straw. 'There's a film on tonight and I need someone to go with.' I tried making out I might have something on, but she said I had nothing of the sort. I made another protest that I may well have something to do, but she just giggled at this. 'Something more important than accompanying me?'

She was hungry, and only for pizza, so we finished our drinks and went to a small pizza parlour at the end of the Alameda. As she ate, I told her about my new studio. She listened and nodded, glancing up as she picked slices of fried eggplant off the pizza topping, eating these separately.

The temperature had dropped and there was a light breeze. As we walked to the film, I felt us sharing a fleeting contentment with life. Clara mentioned how good the pizza had been. I felt a lightness from the beers and whiskey I'd drunk.

We got to a small, winding cobbled street, devoid of people. At this point she looped her arm through mine, not saying anything, just smiling.

The screening was in a large courtyard, a part of the university. We took two chairs near the back. I whispered to Clara, asking which film we were watching. 'They normally show an old film,' she whispered, then told me to be quiet, as it was about to start.

The projection started and Clara shot me a quick smile as the titles to *Breakfast at Tiffany's* appeared. Leaning towards her, I asked her if she'd seen the film. She shook her head gently, her eyes not leaving the screen.

As the film played, I repeatedly glanced from the projection of Audrey Hepburn, across to Clara. She was resting her chin on her hand and kept it there for most of the film. The skin of her forearm had an incredibly soft appearance, evenly tanned and unblemished. If you looked closely enough, you could make out tiny indentations, the little craters of hair follicles. Her eyes flickered across the screen, scanning the subtitles from left to right, the pupils darting, the whites unchanging.

At the end of the film, everybody stood up almost at once, creating a clatter of metal chairs scraping across paving. Clara smiled at me again and we joined the other cinephiles in filing out of the courtyard.

On the way back, she didn't loop her arm through mine and, instead, talked avidly about the film, with large hand gestures. She insisted we walk back past my apartment and I agreed.

We arrived at my door and she looked across the street. Her father knew the owner of the bar opposite, she told me. I invited her up to see the studio, but she said she had to work the next day. 'Another time,' she told me and kissed both cheeks, letting her hand linger on my shoulder.

TWENTY-ONE

EVERY MORNING, I pour myself a cup of the office's tarry filter coffee and walk back to my desk past the stationery cupboard. Here, each day, I take a fresh black biro. Blue seems to make me scrawl, but in black I take more care and, besides, black ink doesn't seem to blot as much as blue.

If I look over my partition, to the right of my computer screen, but to the left of the pot plant on Edith's desk beyond, I can see right across the office, to Laura's desk. Normally, her face is obscured by her monitor, but if she moves her head from behind her screen, occasionally I catch her gaze and she sends me the tiniest wry smile. Her eyes hardly ever leave the screen, though, and, when she does look away, it is usually to accept a pile of files from one of the firm's lawyers.

Today she wears a black cardigan, trimmed with sequins. To me, this detail is tasteless and I find myself thinking back to the simpler cardigan she wore the other day, and regretting that I didn't return her compliment.

I spend the morning considering whether to ask her out for coffee. I'm sure she will say yes, at the very least out of politeness, but when lunchtime arrives, I duck out of the office without her noticing.

After eating at the table by the door at the burrito place, I take an extended wander through the shopping streets. Everyone appears to be a touch happier today for some reason, though I can't figure out quite why.

I find myself in a homeware store, incuriously picking up objects and then placing them back on their shelves. A set of wooden coasters, a model of a stork made from wire, then some scented candles.

An aisle away from me, an old lady with a turned-up nose examines a floral photo frame and then passes it to her friend. The second lady takes a pair of glasses that hang from her neck on string and pushes them to her face. She then turns the frame over in her hands, before holding it at arm's length.

The first lady has picked up another photo frame and is now discussing that. I have stopped where I am, to witness this vapid exchange. I dig my hands into my coat pockets and strain to hear what they are muttering to each other. It is none of my business, I know, but that they should come here to examine photo frames makes me pity them. But this pity only lasts for a moment, before being sharply replaced by self-awareness that it is myself I should judge, spending my lunchtime alone, peering over a homeware store's shelves at a pair of shoppers I have never met, before trudging back to my office to spend the afternoon updating files on clients I have never met either.

I refocus my vision, away from the background of these fussy ladies, to the shelves just in front of me. I stare blankly at a row of bubble bath and scented oils, think briefly of Alyson leant over the edge of that bathtub, then push my hands further into my coat pockets and march out of the store.

TWENTY-TWO

SEÑORA ROSALES HELD the same elegant posture she always did at breakfast. Again she wore her wide-brim hat. I asked what she'd done over the weekend. She told me that she'd been to Cádiz to pass a couple of days by the sea with a friend, to a little secluded beach that could only be reached by a zigzagging path from the coastal road. Her skin looked fresh and healthy, in the way only the salty sea air can make skin appear.

As a thank-you for sorting me out with the apartment, I insisted she come over for a light dinner one evening. She took to this idea, saying that that night would be perfect, as she needed to hand over some apartment keys to a Swedish couple in my part of town at 8pm. She would bring dessert, she added.

I bought two sole from the fishmonger, then visited the grocer with hands like brown paper, collecting lemons, parsley, potatoes and chives. I must have spent nearly half an hour in a small wine shop, first trying to decipher the labels and then indecisively flitting between different bottles. I settled on a chardonnay and handed the shop assistant a five euro bill.

On the way home, I stumbled upon a place that sold gas. It would have been hard to call it a shop – more like a disused garage, with canisters lined up against one wall and a wall-papering table forming a desk. The vendor wore an ill-fitting jumper and jeans covered in grease and oil. His hair was receding, but his goatee was neatly trimmed. I had to make two trips back to the studio: one to return the groceries, the second to heave the canister back, stopping in the street several times to rest my arms, before finally arriving at the studio soaked in sweat.

That afternoon, I took a coffee in the bar with the hatched trellis. I waited until 6pm, but Clara didn't pass by. With little else to do, I read as much as I could of the thriller set in Stockholm. I found myself getting annoyed at the denseness of the main character and that the plot didn't seem to be headed anywhere. Putting this book to one side, I picked up the Benjamin essays. There had once been a cover, but the binding had fallen apart, leaving many of the pages loose. I read a chapter on fashion in 19th-century Paris, then one on boredom. Everything we do, Benjamin surmised from Emile Tardieu's *L'Ennui*, is a vain attempt to escape boredom – yet everything that was, is and will be, appears as the inexhaustible nourishment of that feeling. I turned this over in my mind. I tried to relate this to myself and thought whether it was really boredom I was trying to avoid, sat in the street, in front of an empty coffee cup, waiting for Clara, yet with no arrangement made to meet her. I then thought of her, working at the hostel reception, taking reservations, checking in guests; and then of the sole in the fridge, wrapped in white fishmonger's paper.

Señora Rosales arrived dead on 8.30pm. She had brought a bottle of white wine, too, and a corkscrew, assuming I didn't yet have one in the apartment. She handed me two slices of cheesecake, bought from a dessert counter and loosely wrapped in plastic sheets, telling me to put them in the fridge.

I'd moved the table out onto the rooftop and we laid out what we had. I had cooked the sole simply, in lemon juice and parsley, and served it with boiled potatoes. I complemented Señora Rosales on the wine. She smiled, saying it was her favourite. We talked a little about the business. All her money, she told me, came from northern European holidaymakers, but despite this, they were a people she would never understand. There was a simultaneous openness and falsity about the locals of Sevilla, she said, that made people of most other nationalities seem bland and shallow. She told me about the village she'd grown up in near Sevilla and how she'd moved to the city when she'd married her husband. We didn't talk any more about him.

To emphasise certain points she made, Señora Rosales would lean forward and touch my forearm as it rested on the table. When she began talking about a small bar I should visit, a small bar with climbing wall plants and a rickety old piano, she spoke intensely and took hold of my arm firmly, only releasing it when she had finished her description.

We finished the fish and I cleared the plates. Señora Rosales complimented me on my cooking and we started on the cheesecake. I was feeling a little lightheaded and sleepy due to the wine. As she spoke, I was distracted by a sound from the street, that half-sounded like my neighbour greeting someone. I turned my attention back to our conversation again. Señora Rosales was describing how now, early summer, was the best time of year in Seville, before the nights became unbearably hot in midsummer. She leaned towards me as she spoke and, as she did, her top loosened. My eyes looked into hers, matching the intensity of her gaze, and I only once glanced at her cleavage for the tiniest of moments when I blinked, taking in the curve of each breast, the V of her blouse collar, the angle of her collar bone. Her eyes didn't leave mine, the pupils darting across my face, the whites unchanging. I suddenly became aware of footsteps in the stairwell and glanced over. I looked back at Vicenta, who seemed not to have heard the approaching footsteps at all, and then looked back over her shoulder, towards the stairs again, to see Clara emerge.

Everything froze, except Vicenta. She continued to talk, looking directly at me. I gazed past her, straight at Clara. Clara looked at me, then at Señora Rosales' back, then at her arm stretched out towards mine. Clara didn't say anything, but as she looked back at me, her eyes asked me the most innocent and naked questions possible. They asked me about the film we'd watched together, about how she'd looped her arm through mine as we'd walked. They asked me about this woman opposite me, about the wine glasses and cutlery. About the arm stretched out towards mine. About that first time she'd seen me, when I had arrived tired and grumpy at the reception of her hostel, and how her smile had been enough to persuade me to stay.

Vicenta's speech slowed as she noticed my gaze drift past her. I snapped back into the conversation and Vicenta responded, slowly picking up her pace.

I glanced over her shoulder again, back towards the stairwell, only to see Clara's expression drop away, and by the time I could send another glance her way, she was nowhere to be seen.

TWENTY-THREE

GETTING INTO THE office early to finish a file Robert needs by mid-morning, I take advantage of the empty office to move Edith's pot plant a couple of inches to the right and my computer screen a couple of inches to the left. When Edith eventually gets in at 9am, she doesn't notice, or at least I think she doesn't. Anyway, my line of sight to Laura's desk is slightly less obscured, as is hers to mine.

The top drawer of my desk is beginning to fill with black biros, so once I have finished up the file in question, I set about sorting the contents of the drawer. I create a neat pile of biros and secure them with an elastic band. I then take a pile of redundant documents to the shredder and feed them through one at a time, taking special care that the names and addresses are severed by one of the blades.

Laura has abandoned the sequined cardigan, opting for a white blouse and maroon pullover, much more to my taste. At eleven o'clock, I time my run to the office's kitchenette with hers. She pours herself a cup of the tarry filter coffee, before handing me the pot. I ask her what she did last night. This seemingly sudden interest in her and her life makes her grin and she replies by telling me she went to the cinema. I ask her what film she watched, but I don't recognise the title. She laughs and says I must have seen posters or adverts for it; it's been number one at the box office for a month. I shrug. Feeling the conversation has reached a dead end, I insist I have to get back to work. Laura asks if I'd like to get a coffee at lunch. I think back to my lunch hour standing in the homeware store, gazing blankly at the scented candles and oils, and decide anything would be better than that. We agree to leave at one o'clock. I take my cup of coffee and head back to my desk.

TWENTY-FOUR

I FOUND A sports store and bought the cheapest pair of Nikes they had. At 7am the next day, I got up, threaded the laces and jogged down to the river. I sat on a short wall near the cambered bridge and waited. The sun rose, finally bringing colour to the previously dimly lit riverside. I continued waiting, until further down the bank, I saw the man with greying curls appear. As he got closer, I began stretching my calves from where I sat. Just after he passed me, I got up and began running in the same direction.

We ran south. It wasn't hard to keep to his pace. I watched him plant each foot and synchronised my steps. My Nikes, originally white, quickly became discoloured from the yellowy dust they kicked up. I kept a good twenty metres behind him, knowing I could speed up if he made a turn.

Just after the bridge to Triana, we left the riverbank and ran alongside the road. A long boulevard, lined with palm trees, stretched out endlessly in front of us. The road was nearly empty, the odd bus passing. The buildings became grander and I noticed several embassy signs on gates. We finally reached a cafe on a junction, where a waiter was hauling out plastic tables and chairs. I stopped, placing my hands on my hips, and breathed heavily. The man with greying curls continued. The waiter set four chairs around the table he had just pulled over and looked at me. I looked directly back at him. We stood for a moment, looking at each other. Not a single car passed. He then went to take another table from inside the cafe. I turned around and began running back up the boulevard of embassies. I didn't look back, but couldn't shake the feeling that the waiter had stopped what he was doing again to watch me run off.

I drank two cups of coffee at the small cafe that looked out across the river. A shirtless old man sat on one of the jetties on the other side of the river, fishing. The water was a bluey-green. It was hard to imagine any fish surviving below the surface. The old man looked a little drunk. The sun was out and I could feel it warming every fine hair along my collar.

I continued to flick through the Benjamin essays. Chapters seemed to stop abruptly; whole sections appeared to be missing. A guy and a girl sat two tables away. He had jet-black, curly hair and a whiskery moustache; she wore a beautiful summer dress. She laughed at whatever he said and he smiled heartily when she did. I really couldn't tell if they were romantically involved or not and, without knowing why, this made me happy.

The pages were almost disintegrating in my hands. Benjamin moved on to the flâneur. His flâneur wanders and strolls round 19th-century Paris, a disconnected observer. Benjamin paints him as a distinct member of Parisian street life. He is on its fringes, camouflaged within the crowd. To him, the streets are a theatre, with an ever-more complex cast and plot. The flâneur is the only observing audience member of this play. Maybe there are other flâneurs, at different vantage points, but what they witness would be a completely different work. As the characters of his theatre present themselves only randomly, in flashes, the flâneur is our only possible protagonist, both sociologist and anthropologist, alienated and immersed in his city. He places himself in a different cafe chair, or in a different arcade, and the theatre revolves around him.

Two short, squat ladies took a table in front of me. They sat there waiting, even though there was no table service. They seemed to be bickering about this, about whether to get up and order at the bar. I became annoyed that they had broken my train of thought, but eventually one of them got up. I read on. Benjamin continued on the topic of his flâneur.

'The man flatters himself that, on seeing a passerby swept along by the crowd, he has accurately classified him, seen straight through to the innermost recesses of his soul – all on the basis of external appearance.'

Without knowing why, I thought back to the man with the caramel-coloured suitcase in the guesthouse. I thought back to how I had looked at him, and he had looked at me, with a gaze that had looked straight into me. A couple of moments had been enough and he had returned to his business. I tried to remember what he had returned to. Did he return to paying his board, counting out notes and coins, or had he simply seen enough? Was that one look at me enough for him to assess me, to know me?

There was a chance he was still in the city. I imagined him looking into shop windows, or strolling up the Alameda, sitting at the cafe terraces, his ambivalent observation.

The shirtless man on the jetty had caught something and was reeling it in. The two old ladies still hadn't been served, but had stopped bickering about this. I collected up the pages of the Benjamin, patted my shirt pocket to check my bank card was there, and left.

I crossed the river and walked along the opposite bank. The shirtless man had cast his line again. Some way down the bank, I took a turn away from the river, into Triana. The sun didn't bake these narrower streets in the way it hit the riverbanks. I reached the guesthouse I had stayed at weeks before and leant up against the wall on the opposite side of the street. I could just see through the window of the front door, into the dimly lit lobby. The guesthouse owner was there, behind the desk, speaking to someone on the other side. There was a man opposite her, although I couldn't make out who, as he had his back to me. Come forward, I begged silently, come forward into the light. He didn't. Instead, he turned and headed out of sight, towards the stairs leading to the guesthouse rooms. I could just make out the guesthouse owner taking out her large book and noting something down.

TWENTY-FIVE

As MUNDANE AS it is, I don't dislike my main duty, of keying in figures, as much as you'd think. It takes focus and concentration; it leaves no room for thoughts or worries, only a constant stream of numbers. Fifteen dollars. Seventy-two. One hundred and sixty-eight dollars forty-five. One hundred and thirty. One hundred and thirty. Twelve dollars petty cash. This can go on all afternoon, meaning I only have to return to my life, and all it entails, once I leave this safety net of digits and figures at the end of the day.

My mind begins to wander, however, when Robert asks me to check documents for discrepancies, to seek out the errors in the accounts. The errors are so few and far between, so difficult to notice, that it is easy to lose focus. This morning, he has tasked me with checking off a client's invoices against receipts received. He feels we are two hundred dollars out. I set to work, matching dates to invoice numbers. Everything is matching up, nothing seems awry. The longer I search for the discrepancy, the less likely it seems I will find it. I have to convince myself it exists, otherwise surely Robert wouldn't have asked me to look for it.

Laura has her hair up. As my hope of finding Robert's discrepancy dwindles, I find myself glancing past the computer monitor and Edith's pot plant more and more often. Laura returns a few glances and even shoots me a couple of smiles.

At some point around mid-morning, she collects a pile of documents and heads off to a meeting.

I look back at my computer screen. Something doesn't feel right. I feel overwhelmed, but god knows by what.

I go up to Robert and ask if I can get out for ten minutes, as I need some air. Robert swivels in his chair, looks at his watch and sighs. 'Granville, we can't have everybody leaving when they want to.' He looks at me and asks me if everything is okay. I say everything is fine and get back to work.

At one o'clock, Laura comes and stands by my desk.

'Coming out for lunch, Granville?'

We return to the same coffee shop. Laura tells me about her meeting, but I can't think of much to say. I still haven't shrugged that feeling of being overwhelmed, but I think it better not to mention this. I don't normally take sugar in my coffee, but I feel a little anxious, so decide to add a sachet just to have something to do with my hands. Laura is talking about her tuition and asking how she'll ever be able to pay it back, but I am distracted by a woman in wide-frame sunglasses sitting at the next table, accompanied by her kindergarten-aged daughter. The young girl has a pile of the coffee shop's serviettes, drawing on them in thick felt-tip pen. Every time she wants a new pen, she shouts at her mother, demanding a new colour. Her mother hands each to her brusquely, before returning her attention to her glossy magazine. A cellphone starts buzzing from their direction. The mother huffs as she puts down her magazine, sets out an enormous handbag on the table and begins rummaging through it, looking for the ringing cellphone. The young girl shouts for another colour. The mother glares at her from behind her sunglasses and continues rummaging. In the end, she misses the call. The young girl yells the colour again.

I turn back to Laura and, as I look at her, I try to imagine her with the enormous handbag, the wide-rimmed sunglasses, the pack of felt-tip pens. Of course, she doesn't realise I am doing this, but purely by chance, she sends me a tiny smile as I study her. And just from this, I feel enough at ease to put down the sachet of sugar I've been fidgeting with and smile back.

TWENTY-SIX

I ARRIVED AT Señora Rosales' office five minutes late, to find her waiting at the door. She wasn't at all annoyed and, instead, took my hand briefly and led us down to the cafe on the corner. Once inside, she ordered breakfast for both of us, by then knowing my order as if it were her own. I noticed the bar girl smile as she spoke to Señora Rosales, who then returned to our table and set down her diary and a pile of emails she had printed out for me to reply to.

Over breakfast, I brought up the guesthouse owner. Señora Rosales told me that she knew her well enough, but only through business. 'I sometimes send clients to her if I am overbooked,' she told me. I asked her if she had ever sent a moustached man with a caramel-coloured suitcase to the guesthouse. She looked at me for a moment, gauging my seriousness. 'How would I remember, Granville?'

I returned to my breakfast. Señora Rosales wore two large wooden bracelets on one wrist, which clanked together each time she lifted and then set down her cup of coffee. As she ate, she occasionally adjusted her dress so it continued to cover the tops of her knees.

After breakfast, we went back to her office and worked from there. Señora Rosales left a couple of answerphone messages for clients and I typed up an email for her. Around mid-morning, I asked if I could get out for ten minutes, as I needed some air. Having left the office, I ambled down a couple of streets and then sat down on a doorstep for a few minutes, watching sparrows scrap over some crumbs. When I got back to the office, Señora Rosales wanted to know if everything was okay. I said everything was fine and got back to work.

Later that day I took a seat outside a small bar at the far end of the Alameda, drinking my beers slowly to stretch out the handful of coins I had on me. I smoked and read the loose pages of the Benjamin texts. As the afternoon went on, the bar began to fill, with customers spilling out onto the terrace where I sat. The bargirl turned some music on. The chatter and laughter became so loud I could no longer think. I was hungry, and was just about to leave, when a man in his thirties, already drunk and with a beer-belly squeezed into a tight-fitting Ramones T-shirt, asked me for a light. Hearing my reply, he immediately switched into a drunken, broken English and pulled up a chair at my table without asking.

He asked me where I was from and what I did. A little irritated that he was still clutching my lighter, I kept my answers short. As the bargirl walked past, he reached out and touched her thigh, to stop her. She shot him a dirty look, but he managed to order us each a beer and then offered me a cigarette. I took back my lighter and, having gained a smoke and a beer, felt a little more relaxed. I asked his name. Miguel, he replied, patting his chest.

Miguel asked me if I knew Chuck Berry, rolling the Rs in Berry so much the name seemed unfamiliar. I nodded, swigging back my beer. He proceeded to utter some riffs, semi-tunefully, using his cigarette as an imaginary pick in between drawing on it. He moved onto a Hendrix riff. When he asked me if I knew the songs, I said yes, but only as that was the easier answer.

I gathered my things and left Miguel at his table. I wandered down the Alameda, where by then tables were filling with people drinking in the sun. I took the street with the trellised bar, but didn't give it more than a glance as I passed its tables.

I descended the steps that led down to the river and walked along the bank. Some runners passed me, their faces bloated and swollen red with sweat in the heat. Others let pet dogs run ahead of them, off their leads. The water shimmered, the reeds remained motionless in the thick air. My shirt felt heavy. For each passerby, I wondered why they were out that day and could think of no better reason than the lure of the vivid blue sky that hung serene above the city.

TWENTY-SEVEN

ONE LUNCHTIME, WITH the sun out, we ordered our coffees in corrugated paper take-away cups and took them to the park. The birds were chirping and I definitely felt happy, I'm sure. As we walked round, Laura twice brushed her hand against mine. The first time it happened, I looked down at both our hands, worried I may have stepped too close. The second time, I caught her glance and looked deep into her eyes, before she fluttered her eyelids and looked away again.

We made one lap of the park and then headed for the exit. Just before the gate, she slowed down her walk. I slowed down and stopped, then turned to look at her. Laura leant towards me and, with her hand resting lightly on my upper arm, placed a kiss on my lips. She let her hand linger on my coat sleeve a little longer, before we both turned to face ahead and began walking back.

On this walk back to our office, I felt the same tingle of excitement as I would have done as a teenager. The excitement of liking someone again, of believing that they really wanted to know you, but without knowing what to say to them. Only now, a few years older, I found that giddiness uncomfortable, so uncomfortable that I should feel even a touch intoxicated by this faux connection. We took the elevator up to our floor in awkward silence. When we headed to our separate desks, I made sure I gave her a smile, which she returned. I then sat down and began to concentrate on my work, without looking past my computer screen, or past the pot plant on Edith's desk.

Later that night, I searched for Alyson's name on the internet. There were several results I knew weren't her – an Alyson Jennings in Australia, then an outdoor activities instructor in Maine. I found one reference to her name on an agency website in Chicago. It consisted only of a contact name and number, with no photo, so I couldn't be sure it was her. I kept scrolling down, but there was no more information. Without really knowing why, I jotted the number down on a scrap of paper, before switching the computer off.

TWENTY-EIGHT

A MORNING HAS passed, of which I remember nothing, other than flitting between my desk and my bed, sitting and lying, and it is only when the thought of my life slipping through my fingers – slipping away while I do nothing but stare at the ceiling – crosses my mind that I leave the studio and run to the street.

To travel and to see the world is to validate oneself, one's existence. He who travels needs no sense of purpose, as purpose is presented to him every step of the way, by each journey, by each new experience. That airline ticket or that rail pass is direction – direction itself – as well as being an excuse for not having any in your own life. But you must never stay too long, or that direction fades. To find yourself settled is to find yourself asked those same questions as before. Having escaped where you left, that new life has direction, but what you can never escape is what drove you away.

And it is only today, as I shuffle as quickly as I can through the streets of the city, keeping out of the way of passersby as much as I try to keep out of the sun, that I really think back to Madison. Really think back: not just let a memory flicker, then push it immediately from my mind as soon as it starts to bud. It is only today that I really picture the desk I should be sat at, the office where I should be, the life I should be building. Of working hard and, if not that, working and saving. And it is now that I realise that by blocking every thought I've had of Alyson these last couple of months, I have never wondered where she is and what she might be doing. And when I ask myself this, I realise I no longer have any notion of what one might achieve in four months, of where one can get to, and I have no idea how far she has got in those months since I last saw her. I have lived without planning or thinking. I have sat and watched, from cafes and park benches, and even in the little work I do for Señora Rosales, it is as if I have been employed as little more than a passive observer, an audience member to her business, given a place to sit and look over whatever she puts in front of me.

And as I dash though the narrow, crowded streets of the city, I become increasingly overwhelmed. The people are too many. It is not only this, though: with every person, with every glance I catch, I am hit by their 'doing': not what they are doing, or if they are even aware of it, but the very fact they are going about their lives unhindered; it is simply that when I catch their glance, I am met by some meaning to life. Men dressed in suits, their jackets flung over their shoulders due to the heat, marching steadily to their next meeting. Teenagers, gawping through shop windows then collapsing onto each other in fits of laughter that I will never understand. Mothers stopping strollers as they bump into friends, before both women lean over to coo over the children inside. And whether this meaning is actually there behind their eyes, or whether it is something I have assigned by myself, is not important. The only thing I feel is the void inside myself where something should be and it makes my eyes well with tears. It is one thing to see every man and woman, obliviously carrying their own meaning, going about their lives, but it is quite another that even when that meaning is there in front of me, head-on, it fails to resonate with me.

I need to sit, but do not pull up a chair at one of the cafes where people amble by. I am almost at the point of breaking into a run when I finally find an alley to duck into, completely shaded by overhanging buildings, free of people. I sit down on a doorstep and steady my breathing. Whatever Alyson is doing now, I convince myself, will be so much more meaningful than this. I am made to wince, as even though I have no idea what she has ended up doing, I know that the drive she has and her urge to better herself will have taken her somewhere. She will have been hired by some top firm, submerged in meetings and deadlines, thriving in such a situation. And most probably it was that same drive that told her to end things with me, the same drive that could see I was destined for such a state of limbo, the same drive that won through and took her away from me. My breathing steadies and I release the grip I had on my knees. I am washed by a defeated calm. Because whatever drove her away from me was right to do so. Neither the odd morning's work with Señora Rosales, nor the infrequent, chance encounters I have with Clara, are any way to measure a life. I pick myself up, walking home more slowly and heavily than before. I realise I have tricked myself into thinking that all this around me is a life, that these en-counters mean something. As I walk, I look into the eyes of passersby, hoping that now, out of my earlier hysterical state, I will see something. Yet with each stare, there is nothing I can appreciate. The faces run out and the streets wind and twist towards my apartment – until, utterly exhausted, I stumble into my room, which receives me with a cold air.

TWENTY-NINE

ALMOST WITHOUT REALISING, I have started going out with Laura. I stop going to the burrito place at lunch. Instead, we spend our breaks together in the coffee shop. Even when I am in moods where I don't have anything to say, she manages to get something out of me and I end up laughing with her, or at least smiling.

I like having something to do on a Friday night after work, hanging out with someone and not really having to worry about stuff. A couple of Fridays running, we go to a cocktail lounge on West Main Street that Laura has introduced me to. Each time, I tell Mom I'll be back home late from the office, without saying why. She doesn't ask either, just like she didn't ask about Alyson. Inside the bar, Laura tries a few cocktails from the menu: a daiquiri, a cosmopolitan. I stick to beer. At the end of the night, we walk to the taxi rank, make out for a while waiting for a cab and then head home in separate directions. Sometimes we hang out again on the Saturday, but I haven't got round to getting a cellphone yet, so it's difficult to meet up. Other than that, I don't think about her too much until we see each other Monday morning.

On one Sunday afternoon, I find myself alone in the house. I think about calling Laura on the house phone, but instead, I enter the kitchen and open the fridge. I am not really hungry, but I set about making myself a ham and turkey sandwich. I cut the sandwich diagonally, then fold up and seal the packets of cold meats and return them to the fridge. I think about having a Coke, but instead choose to run myself a glass of water.

Flicking through cable channels, I find the Brewers game on Fox. I lay my plate on the arm of the sofa and stare into the television, reaching for my sandwich, taking a bite and then setting it back down. The sandwich is a little dry, as I haven't put enough mayonnaise on the bread, and I gulp down my glass of water rather more quickly than I would normally. I cannot be bothered to pour myself another glass, so leave the last piece of sandwich untouched.

With the Brewers one up, the house phone begins to ring. I wonder if it is Laura. I can't remember if she said she'd call. I stare at the phone as it rings. I should get up to answer it, but without knowing why, I stay where I am.

I continue staring at the phone from the sofa. The longer I stare, the less the sound seems to be coming from the phone. As it continues to ring and ring, I begin to observe the phone as nothing more than an inanimate object: a case of plastic; the curve of the receiver; the tangled cord. After a few more rings, the caller gives up. I return to the game and my sandwich.

THIRTY

S EÑORA ROSALES HAD not arrived and the office shutters were closed. The corner of an envelope poked out from under the door, showing the postman had been. I slid the letter out. It was a statement from the bank. I folded it, pushed it into my back pocket and headed two doors down, to the cafe we sometimes worked in.

Even on the days we did work in the cafe, Señora Rosales would at least open up the office beforehand. The cafe was nearly empty, save an older gentleman, reading the newspaper, and two ladies sat near the back, talking rapidly in hushed tones. The young waitress busied herself turning bread under the grill.

I stood in the doorway for a moment, deciding whether to stay or head back to the office. Señora Rosales would at least check here when she arrived. I decided to enter and pulled up a stool next to the bar. The waitress had left the grill and was plating a *tostada*. She smiled at me and asked me what I wanted.

Maybe I had got the day wrong. I took a newspaper to check the date. It was a Wednesday, the day I worked. My *tostada* came out. The waitress passed me the oil and salt, and returned to the coffee machine. The gentleman next to me folded his newspaper and began counting out some change. He placed this on his saucer. 'Carmen . . .' he called to the waitress, before pointing to the coins, then leaving.

The owner of the cafe emerged from a door behind the bar.

I had seen him here a few times before, sometimes serving customers himself, sometimes adding up till receipts with a stubby pencil that he kept in his shirt pocket. The waitress asked him about something. As she was speaking, he shot me a glance and then whispered something under his breath. She turned, glanced at me and nodded. The cafe owner then disappeared through the door he'd entered.

I raised my coffee to my mouth, without drinking it. My fingers smelt of old cigarettes. I took a sip, then placed the cup back on its saucer, keeping my eyes on the door behind the bar, where the cafe owner had disappeared.

Moments later, he reemerged. He squeezed past the waitress, who was back at the grill, and came to my end of the bar. Leaning forwards, he placed his clenched hands on the bar and let his weight fall on them.

'Granville?' he pronounced. I gave the smallest nod. He explained something quickly in Spanish, without me following a word. He then opened one of his hands and pushed a set of keys into mine. I said nothing. He gestured towards the door. I nodded, to feign understanding, but remained lost in the exchange. The cafe owner then shrugged his shoulders and walked away.

The two ladies came up to the bar to pay. I looked at the keys the cafe owner had forced onto me. One long and slightly rusty, the other a short door key. I took a handful of coins from my pocket, counted out enough to cover my breakfast and left.

The keys were, as was my only guess, the keys to Señora Rosales' office. The shorter key unlocked the front door with one turn and unlatched it with a second.

I'd never entered the office alone before. Señora Rosales would always have arrived beforehand, busying herself with paperwork, or sitting at her computer.

The office was almost pitch black with the shutters closed. I fumbled around at the windows for the latch. Releasing it suddenly drenched the room in sunlight, stirring the air, flecks of dust floating upwards in flows and currents.

I sat at Señora Rosales' desk. There were two neat piles of documents – one squared to the left, one to the right – and three pens lined up in the middle: two biros and a fountain pen. I tried the long key in the desk drawer, but it didn't fit. I took the folded envelope containing the bank statement from my back pocket and placed it on the desk.

It was then I noticed the top sheet on the right pile of documents had my name on it. I took it from the pile and placed it in front of me. The message was hastily written, on the same thick cream paper that Señora Rosales' original advert had been.

Granville,
As you will see, I can't be here.
I hope you find the keys with Francisco next door.
Mother is ill. I have gone to Extremadura.
The diary on the desk has all the bookings.
Don't worry about making any more at this time.
Vicenta

I turned the note over. The back was blank. That was it. No further details, no timescale.

I brought the diary towards me. Señora Rosales hadn't mentioned her mother before. Nothing about ill health, nothing even about her as a person. The pages of the diary were a stark white, marked only with the names, numbers and apartments that her clients had booked by the day they were to arrive, all in her immaculate handwriting. There were six arrivals due this week. I tucked Señora Rosales' note into the diary, took the diary under my arm and headed out, locking up the office behind me.

THIRTY-ONE

GETTING HOME FROM work, after a day in which nothing really happened, I go to the bathroom, run the tap and drench my face in cold water. Turning off the tap, I look into the mirror, press my cheekbones curiously, then pat my face dry. Both Mom and Dad are out, Dad still at work, Mom god knows where.

I go and sit on my bed. Looking out of my window, I trace the lines of the tree branches. A number of birds land, look around, then fly off again. The last of them fly away and I bring my attention back to where I am sat.

In the corner of the room, there are two cardboard boxes, sealed with packing tape, containing old possessions. I go over. From the weight of one, I know it is nothing more than books. With a key, I slice open the packing tape on top of the other. Inside, there is an envelope of photos that I decide not to sift through and two T-shirts - a Brewers tee from when I was 12 or so and an old summer camp tee. From beneath these, I pull out a pair of high-top trainers, a pair of Nikes Air Force Ones. They are a little scuffed, but look my size. I lace them up and walk around the room. With nothing to do, I take my packet of cigarettes and head out of the house.

I wander aimlessly across Madison. The traffic is thick at this hour. A long queue forms at the supermarket parking lot. For seven o'clock, it's still warm. Main Street and Washington Avenue still buzz with people, leaving work late, meeting friends, the men in T-shirts or with rolled-up shirt sleeves, the women in blouses or sleeveless tops. There are too many people here for me to sit and have a beer alone, I decide. Tenney Park isn't too far off, I tell myself, and, besides, the walk will stretch my legs.

Away from the hubbub of cars and people, I feel somewhat calmed. My breathing slows, as does my pace. I take the path by Lake Mendota, crossing the tiny beach, letting one foot drag after the other. Middle-aged men are out with their dogs. An occasional couple pass, some talking and smiling, others pressing forward in silence. The air is fresher here, amongst the trees and beside the water. It's not the sea air of Portbou, where the salt tickles your nostrils, but breathing deeply, I feel alive, or at the very least, conscious.

There is an iron bridge which crosses an estuary of sorts, a stream coming from Lake Mendota and cutting into the park. Stopping halfway, I lean over the edge and stand my left foot on the railings. I light a cigarette and, inhaling the first puff of smoke, push my foot out, and stare at the upper of the Nike dangling over the water. When I look up, I realise the sun has started setting and the sky is tinged pink. For a moment, I forget that I have to go to the office tomorrow; I forget that maybe I should have called Laura this evening; I forget that Alyson has yet to call me and never explained what I had done wrong. The sunlight dims a little more and I take my foot from the railings, start walking home and return to worrying about all that I momentarily forgot.

THIRTY-TWO

THE PHONE RANG again. I hadn't answered it for days. Answering phones calls would only mean more clients, something I couldn't stomach. I gave it five rings for the caller to give up, but it continued. I stared at it as it rang, staring at it as an object: a case of plastic; the flat, rectangular receiver; the tangled cord. As it rang and rang, it occurred to me it could be Señora Rosales. Why else would this caller be so persistent? What if it had been her trying to get through for the last few days? I placed my hand on the receiver. Things would only get better were she here. I could barely look after myself, let alone this business.

I took a deep breath, then took my hand off the receiver. One phone call wouldn't change anything. If she came, she came, if she didn't, she didn't. It would only be some loved-up French couple on the other end of the line, calling for an apartment near the centre, a romantic getaway. If not, some middle-aged German couple with stroppy kids, demanding things of me their whole vacation. I stared at the phone until it stopped ringing, and left the office.

THIRTY-THREE

I HAVE BEEN waiting at the door of one the apartments for an hour and a half, clutching only Señora Rosales' diary and one of her biros. Finally, a taxi pulls up. The driver opens both doors and helps an old couple out of the cab, before heaving two large suitcases from the trunk.

On the way up the stairs, the husband, an old Austrian gentleman, explains there had been a delay at the airport, although he does so without apologising.

I open up the apartment. It is clean and tidy, but smells a little musty. The husband puts down the suitcases. There is a moment's silence between the three of us which makes me feel I have already overstayed my welcome. I push the set of keys into his hand. He says nothing.

I say I will be on my way, to let them settle in, but as I say this they look at me as if I have forgotten to mention something. I have no idea what they expect me to say. I ask when they would like me to pick up the keys.

'Tuesday,' says the husband.

I nod and leave.

THIRTY-FOUR

I SPENT AN hour in the bar where Miguel had accosted me, playing his cigarette Hendrix. It was a quiet early afternoon for the bar: a couple of pensioners; a student working on her laptop; a different clientele to those here before. I took a final swig of my beer, paid up and left for my studio.

As I climbed my building's stairs, I heard flamenco playing from the first-floor apartment, either a CD or the radio. Over the past few weeks I'd often seen a woman in her thirties, supposedly single, pass me at the building's entrance. I had guessed it was her who lived on the first floor, but couldn't be sure.

Arriving at the studio, I pocketed my corkscrew and promptly left. I headed to the supermarket, took a two-euro bottle of red, paid and headed for Señora Rosales' office.

There were two small coffee cups in the office. I opened the wine, poured myself a cup and sat at her desk. Taking her diary, I leafed through it, searching for an address, a phone number, a clue – anything to tell me where she was, when she'd be back. There was nothing. I poured another cup, gulped it down and poured another. I was starting to feel how stuffy the office was, but didn't want to open the shutters. The air felt thick, yet the sliver of light that broke through the *persianas* was all I could bear.

On my sixth coffee cup of wine, the phone rang. I slowly

finished the wine, but it continued to ring. I looked at the touch-tone pad, slowly counting all ten numbers, the hash and the asterisk. The phone rang incessantly. It has to be her, I told myself. I pushed my coffee cup away and reached for the phone.

'Hello?' I answered.

'Ahhh, hallou . . .' The voice was male and sounded Dutch, or German maybe. 'Apartmentos Rosales?' he asked.

It wasn't her. It was just another client, calling to book an apartment. Señora Rosales' diary was open in front of me. I wanted to know when she was coming back, not when another guest would arrive. I slammed the diary shut.

'Hallou, we'd like to reserve . . .'

'Stay where you are - stay in your country!' Without re-alising it, I was shouting - 'Stay in your country and don't leave!' - shouting so much the line must have distorted.

'Pardon? Is this Apartmentos Rosales?' he almost begged.

I composed myself. 'You have the wrong number,' I gulped. Shaking, I slowly pulled the phone away from my ear and placed the handset on the desk in front of me. The distant sound of his voice continued to call faintly through the speaker. 'Hallou? Hallou?' I could just about hear a click. He'd hung up. I left the phone on the table, so it wouldn't ring again.

Walking beside the river, I took the path down to one of the small jetties and perched on its edge. I looked down at my canvas shoes and swung my feet over the glistening water. I ran my hands over my jeans pockets: only the impression of a bank card, about a euro in change and the keys to the studio. I thought back to the steel bench in Portbou and my cellphone on the seabed. A fish must have swum beneath me, as a few bubbles burst on the water's surface.

In all this time, I'd barely thought of my parents. I'd never thought of how worried they'd be, of why I'd never called. I'd become transfixed by nearly everything else, spacing my days with those chance meetings with Clara, displaced and disorientated by the sudden disappearance of Señora Rosales, crushed by my obsession with how Alyson would have moved on so effortlessly without me. And in that instant – with my feet still swinging above the glistening water – in that instant, all the charm, beauty and sunshine of this city seeped away and I felt an emptiness as if it were as deep as the ocean between me and home. I hunched my legs up, pulled myself up from the jetty and trudged home.

I woke the next morning and lay in the sunlight breaking through the studio window. Judging that I'd already missed most of the morning, I decided it wasn't worth wasting an afternoon in the folds of the sheets as well, and pulled on a T-shirt and jeans without showering. I passed a cashpoint, then perused a few bars, looking for one that would serve an early lunch, and settled on a simple-looking restaurant, with wooden tables in the sun. I ordered a beer and skimmed the menu. When the waiter came out with a *caña*, I sent him back for Russian salad, a tapa of cheese, and pork in whiskey. By the time he'd returned a second time with my food, I'd finished the first beer.

While I was eating, I remembered trudging back home from the jetty the day before. I recalled my train of thought: the breaking bubbles, the bench in Portbou, Clara, Alyson and lastly the realisation that I hadn't called my parents in months. I went over these thoughts, in order, again and again. Everything came back to me, up until the point of that wrenching emptiness. I picked at the Russian salad. Why could I recall – why could I feel – everything, only up until that point? I'd been on the brink of despair the day before, yet today I couldn't feel it: I couldn't recapture its weight.

I chewed the pork slowly, finished off the cheese and gulped down the dregs of my second beer. I was feeling a little sleepy and, besides, the sun was giving me a headache, so I counted out enough to cover my bill and headed back to my studio.

THIRTY-FIVE

I T WAS MONDAY morning and Robert hadn't arrived yet. At some time mid-morning, I asked Edith where he was. He had called in sick, she told me. I nodded and headed back to my desk, but not before I caught Laura's glance. She smiled and I attempted a smile back, but felt my face wrinkle awkwardly, because if there is ever a time I find it difficult to smile, it's Monday morning. I thought about going over to explain this, but instead decided to go and sit back at my desk.

It momentarily crossed my mind that maybe Robert could be faking illness, maybe to spend the day with his children, to extend his weekend a little. But, recalling his normal expressionless look, the short, curt answers he always gave me and that unbreakable gaze into his computer monitor, I quickly realised this couldn't be the case. His was a life dedicated to earning money for his children, not spending time with them and, even if he were to deny this as theory, if he were to say his ideals were far from this, it was at least true in practice. His dedication to his children was one from his office desk and, at least, when he returned home every evening, sapped of energy, he knew the paycheck that would arrive at the end of every month would feed them, clothe them and take them skiing once or twice a year.

At quarter to one, Laura collected me from my desk and we went to lunch. We sat at a small table, in two miniature armchairs, with two coffees in corrugated paper cups and two triangular sandwiches in triangular packets in front of us. Laura was unusually quiet, so I had to make most of the conversation. Doing so made me realise that she was far better at making conversation than I was, which made me feel a little embarrassed and then a little annoyed. I wondered if something was troubling her, but didn't ask. I then began thinking about the burrito place, of sitting at the square table near the door, of my lunches alone, my only interaction with the shop owner, who had learned my name. I looked down at my triangular sandwich. Laura asked me how my work was going. I didn't really feel like saying, but it was better than letting the conversation go stale. I tried to make it sound a little more important than it was, and mentioned that Robert was off sick. Then, in place of asking her if anything was the matter, I complimented her on her top, even though I didn't like it that much.

THIRTY-SIX

I WRENCHED OPEN the shutters of Señora Rosales' office. Again, flecks of dust seemed to float upwards, in flows and currents, dancing in the sunlight.

Getting rid of the telephone was a little more complicated than I had anticipated. The cabling passed through some kind of square, plastic piping behind the desk, which then ran towards some sockets on the wall. I stood for a moment, studying the set-up, before grabbing a biro and cracking open the plastic casing. With a sharp tug, the cable started to reel in.

A row of box files lined the shelf above. I took down the nearest, labelled *Mayo 2011*, and emptied the contents onto the desk: receipts, invoices, printed correspondence, a few Post-it notes. The file itself had a kind of greeny, marbley, tortoise-shell effect, an artefact from several decades before. I placed the phone, with its cable coiled round itself, into the empty box and reshelved it. An odd sense of closure enveloped me. That act – that disconnection – would be the end of Austrian couples standing awkwardly at the entrance of their rented holiday apartments, blank looks across their faces; no more barked enquiries about peak season availability from Holland; no further afternoons sat at Señora Rosales' desk, drinking my way through a bottle of wine, coffee cup by coffee cup, expecting that call from Extremadura that would never come.

A small metal key cabinet was affixed to the wall next

to the door. Inside, about ten sets of keys, each numbered, each with a street name on the key ring. On the bottom right hook, a whole bunch of keys, all attached to the same single key ring, surely her master set. Each key was numbered, each corresponding to a numbered key within the cabinet. All except one. I unhooked the master set, pocketed one of Señora Rosales' business cards from her desk and closed up the office.

THIRTY-SEVEN

ROBERT IS BACK at work. Mid-morning, I go to his office, clutching a pile of purchase orders for him to sign off. While he sifts through the pile, I ask him how his weekend was, just so as not to have to stand there in silence. He mutters something about the weather. He doesn't mention his children, nor does he mention being that ill. I take the signed copies back from him and head towards the photocopier, leaving without any conclusive evidence of where he might have been the day before.

Laura is already at the copier. She flashes me a smile. There's a tiny sparkle in her eye, obviously unintended, but I catch it all the same.

As invisible as these lines are, Laura knows the limits of professionalism, the constraints of circumstance. The flashed smile was little more than she might give to any other co-worker. But for us, such details – a stolen smile, a meeting of eyes – touch on subtext, a subtext only we know. In that moment, with the two of us standing either side of the copier, I am caught wondering if I am at all able to convey the same to her, if my gestures allude to that same something we have, or if she receives my signals in the same way as the stale, icy rapport we all share in this office.

Laura feeds another document into the top of the copier and asks me what I did last night. I imagine the braches of the tree outside my bedroom window, the birds landing one by one, the baseball falling again and again into my hand. 'Not much,' is all I can muster. If I were quicker, I could have recalled some film I'd seen last week, or some book I'd once read.

Laura takes her copies and slides them through her hands atop the machine, to straighten them out.

'I'll catch you later, Granville,' she says, smiling. The sparkle in her eye has gone, but she was never in control of that anyway.

The purchase orders have to be filed away in date order. Shelves of box files line the far end of the office. I sort the orders into piles and pull down their respective tombs. A box file on the bottom shelf catches my eye. It has a kind of tortoiseshell effect and a worn label, with *May 2011* written in faded ink. I stand for a moment, staring at it, a little confused by its allure. Checking nobody is looking, I pull it out. Oddly, holding it before me, it feels far heavier than the other files, as if some foreign object may be present. I click it open and begin to rifle through.

Purchase orders, invoices, a few printed-off reconciliations. Nothing more. With the file cradled in one arm, my other hand now pushing its entirely predictable contents back into order, I can no longer remember what I had expected to find. I close it up and place it back on the shelf.

THIRTY-EIGHT

IT'S MID-AFTERNOON WHEN I get to Avenida de la Buhaira. I stand in front of an apartment block and double-check the address on Señora Rosales' business card.

It must be twenty minutes or so since I last saw anyone on the city's sidewalks. The supermarkets have emptied, the last few ingredients for lunch having been picked up an hour ago. The school gates have closed, mothers and fathers having been and gone, their kids having traipsed behind them as they headed home. Pigeons still peck at the baked earth, seeking leftover crumbs under empty park benches. I sift through the cluster of keys in my hand, pinching that unnumbered key between my fingers and letting the rest slip down the key ring.

The entrance consists of a small foyer. A marble effect covers the walls, floor and ceiling. A couple of large pot plants stand in different corners. The oppressive heat of the street has disappeared, but the same humidity stifles the air.

I take the stairs to the third floor. The apartment door is right at the end of the landing. Upon reaching it, I lean in towards the door with my ear. Not a sound. I try the same unnumbered key in the lock. It clicks open.

A deep red light fills the apartment, the sun beating against the drawn curtains. There are no immediate clues to someone having left in a hurry. Every surface of every unit shines pristinely. Dining chairs are tucked under the table. The sofa cushions have been plumped.

I look down at my scuffed Nikes. Not wanting to leave any trace of my visit, I slip them off and slide them underneath a cast-iron table by the door. A telephone sits on top. My mind is drawn back to that very first conversation with Señora Rosales, conducted over the phone. I imagine her next to the table, phone in one hand, the other forcing on her own shoe with a stamp.

Venturing further into the apartment, I begin to peruse. A particularly large unit spans one wall, lined with ornaments, crockery and a few bookshelves. My eye scans each row. Novels by Cortázar, poetry by Bécquer.

I begin pulling down any spine that in any way resembles an address book. The first is a blank, unused notebook. The next, a double-leafed book of receipts, dating back to the mid-nineties. Continuing along the shelf, I come to a box, stood upright. I slide it out and place it on the display top of the unit. Inside, I find a thick wad of bills – twenties, fifties . . . a bill of two hundred, even. I instinctively count the pile. Some twelve hundred euros.

I make my way through to the apartment's bathroom. Standing in front of the mirror, I run the tap and push my hands under the stream. The water starts off lukewarm, but quickly cools as colder water is drawn up from below the building. Cupping my hands, I begin to splash my face repeatedly. I stare into the mirror. Droplets dot my face. Those twelve hundred euros race around my mind. A train ticket as far as those funds would take me. A few months' rent, a little space of my own. I turn off the tap and pat my hands dry on the hand towel, doing my best not to crease it in any way.

Back in the lounge, I tuck the money back into its box and replace it on the bookshelf. I slip on my shoes, leave the apartment and lock the door behind me.

THIRTY-NINE

I TOOK THE 67 down to West Towne Mall. Eighth-graders filled the bus, goofing about, bickering, poking cellphones and craning over each other to see whatever so-and-so had sent back. In the end I got off a couple of stops early. Better the walk than the suffocation.

In the mall, I half-heartedly browsed a few clothes shops. A bomber jacket momentarily took my fancy. Between two fingers, I began to massage the sleeve material. The nylon slipped right through my grip, the sleeve falling away. I walked away, not bothering to check the price tag.

I joined the queue at the pretzel stand. Two girls stood in line in front of me, staring at their cellphones. There was a college-aged guy at the counter, all pleasantries and white teeth. I told him it'd just be a pretzel and sweet mustard. He picked up on my tone and didn't say anything else until he'd finished wrapping up the pretzel in a paper bag. I rounded the bill up to the nearest buck and walked off.

I found a bench in one of the mall's atriums. A fountain shot up from the middle, with gleaming, fake ferns dotted around the centrepiece.

From the paper bag, I tore off a chunk of the pretzel and began chewing it slowly. Currents of shoppers flowed past, from the entrances of the mall to the arcades, from sports retailers to burger joints, out of the electronics shops and into the computer game stores. I caught a glimpse of the eighth-graders who were on the bus, the girls dragging reluctant boys into a clothes store. A three-year-old, pushed along in a stroller, threw his blanket overboard, sending his mother back to retrieve it. Shifting their weight awkwardly from foot to foot, men stood bored as their partners browsed rails of womenswear, trying their best to look even more indifferent than they actually were.

I sat there for what must have been half an hour. Caught up in their weekend shopping, not one person looked my way, not one caught my eye. The arcades of the mall formed a theatre, the cast as tired as the plot, the characters presenting themselves only in flashes. Before long, each disappeared: to the shops at the other end of the mall, perhaps; outside, to their waiting cars, to fill the trunks with the day's purchases; to the very same pretzel stand I had found myself at, maybe, leaving with a small paper bag folded at the top and a paper ramekin of sweet mustard to carry alongside.

FORTY

I SPRING UP sharply, unaware I have fallen asleep, and take a moment to get my bearings. My bed sheets have come loose at one end and are crumpled up beneath me. I don't remember falling asleep, but it must have been some time after finishing and clearing away my lunch. I go to the studio balcony and look down to the street. It is dusk already and the passageways are beginning to fill. The old waiter in the cafe opposite is clearing away glasses and plates.

There is some wine left open from two nights before on the desk. I pour a short glass. The first gulp is sour and acidic, but I finish the glass, before heading down into the streets.

I find a small plaza that I have passed before, but have never sat in. Here, there are two bars facing each other. One is tiled on the inside, with a long stainless steel bar and a handful of metal tables outside. It is half-full, of couples and families. I see one woman emerge from inside the bar with a large plate of shrimp. The other bar has a neat row of small wooden tables and is empty, apart from a young couple at the end table.

I take a seat at one of these wooden tables. A waiter comes out immediately. I order a beer and a dish each of anchovies and potatoes. He returns promptly with my beer and a basket of bread. The couple share a bottle of white wine. They are clearly on a first date. She seems unrelaxed, whilst he is sitting upright, almost too upright, scared of making the slightest faux pas. He fixes a nervous smile. The waiter brings out my anchovies and I turn my attention away from this couple.

A tall man comes into the square, walking slowly, with his hands clasped behind his back, yet his gaze fixed ahead. As he gets closer, I am taken aback when I realise this is the moustached gentleman from the guesthouse, the one who carried the caramel-coloured suitcase. I silently put down my fork and take a sip of my beer. He is approaching the very restaurant that I am sat outside.

He carefully pulls out a chair and steps between it and the table. He lightly tugs the sides of his trousers to straighten them, and takes his seat. The waiter brings out a bottle of red wine and a single glass. The gentleman tastes the wine, before nodding to the waiter in agreement. Through all this, he does not look across at me, nor at the couple on a date.

I try not to glance over, at least not too often. The gentleman appears quite happy sitting alone, looking out across the square.

He finishes his first glass of wine and then turns to me. 'Do you mind if I smoke?' I am again taken aback, both by this coincidence and his politeness. I shake my head. He takes out a cigarette and points the packet towards me, to offer me one. I feel I could do with a smoke, but shake my head.

I focus on my food. The fried anchovies have gone cold, but the potatoes still have some heat. I take a small scoop from each plate and eat them together.

The gentleman is finishing his second glass of wine when a woman joins him. She has her hair tied back tightly in a bun and wears a dark dress, with floral detail. She is forty or so, I tell myself. The waiter brings out another glass and, as soon as he has, the moustached gentleman pours her a glass of wine, then reclines again in his chair. She doesn't speak and, instead, takes a metal case from her handbag, withdrawing her own slim cigarette. The gentleman offers her a light.

They sit in silence. Her gaze is fixed on a spot on the table near the stem of the wine glass. His bottom lip is twitching a little, as if he is chewing it from the inside. He reaches for her hand on the table and cups it for a moment, before she pulls it away and rests it on her handbag. The gentleman repositions himself in his chair.

The waiter comes out, to the table of the awkward young couple, who by now have given up speaking to each other. He starts gathering up their plates and, sensing the discomfort of their silence, asks them how their food was. The relieved young man jumps straight into conversation, his date remaining as mute as she had been before. As this most mundane of tragicomedies unfolds, I notice the woman with the moustached gentleman has begun to speak to him, although without making eye contact. I strain to hear what they are saying, to catch any tone or inflection of speech that might reveal what he has done – what she has done – what either of them has done – but everything is drowned out by the waiter's clumsy conversation and clearing of the table. The gentleman is nodding. Something is being agreed. I cannot make out a single sound for the racket being played out a table or two down. When I look back, the gentleman is shaking his head and now it is him who is refusing to make eye contact.

'Granville,' a voice whispers. I ignore it. The moustached gentleman's date is holding back her tears. He is still shaking his head and, looking down at his pocket, pulls out his packet of cigarettes. He takes one out, far more abruptly than before.

'Granville.' The voice becomes louder, before it snaps. 'Granville!'

I turn to the voice. Clara is leaning over me. She gives me a gentle, warm smile. A summer dress hangs loosely from her shoulders, where, off one, a small carry-all is slung, and, near the other, her name badge is still clipped. 'What are you doing?' she asks.

I semi-motion towards the plates in front of me to indicate I've eaten and muster enough of a sentence to ask her the same.

'I've just finished work,' she confirms. As she says this, she realises her name badge is still on and begins to unpin it. 'Look, I didn't even notice.' She unhooks it and tucks it into the carry-all. 'Are you waiting for anyone?' I unintentionally leave an unnatural pause before saying I have eaten alone. Clara eyes me cautiously. I apologise and repeat that I'm not waiting for anyone, hopefully a little more convincingly. This makes her smile.

'If you've finished, why not come for a drink with me?' she asks. I nod, wanting to display I am keen, but my attention isn't solely with her. My gaze is drifting to the table across from us, to the moustached gentleman and the woman with him. The waiter has returned inside; there is no longer the clatter of crockery and cutlery. The young couple on a date have returned to their awkward silence. The woman has stopped speaking. She is staring directly at the gentleman, squinting her eyes with a look between disgust and disbelief. 'Are you coming then, Granville?' Clara repeats.

I nod again. I sense I am coming across as shifty, but I can't pull myself away from the situation at the table across from us. Without her becoming agitated, I can feel Clara getting impatient. I take out a five euro bill and start counting out some coins to cover my food. My eyes are darting between Clara and the gentleman at the other table. The woman is taking a pack of tissues from her handbag. I glance around for the waiter, in order to pay up, but he is nowhere to be seen. Clara is itching to get going. I scoop up the money I've collected and head into the bar to pay. When I reemerge, the gentleman and the woman have disappeared, leaving only a pair of wine glasses and a half-finished bottle of red. I am about to ask Clara what happened, where they have gone, in which direction. But seeing her motion to start moving, I realise she probably hasn't noticed and, more so, hasn't cared. We start walking.

Clara suggests we go back to her apartment, as she has to drop off her belongings there. When we arrive, she adds that we might as well eat something too. She lays out two glasses and takes a quart bottle of beer from the fridge. I sit at a small table in the corner of the kitchen, as she moves from cupboard to cupboard, collecting ingredients and placing them on the table in front of me. She then pulls up her own chair and starts slicing tomatoes into a shallow dish, pressing the knife through each fruit until it reaches her thumb on the other side. She takes an avocado, proceeding to peel it in a way I've never seen, as if it were an apple. As she slices the peeled avocado into the same dish, she catches me staring at her and asks me what's up. I shrug and she continues. She coats the dish in olive oil and salt, and places a fork on either side of the plate.

'I'm sorry that it's not much,' she tells me. I say that it doesn't matter as I've already eaten and normally I am happy with whatever I get. She smiles at me like I have said the wrong thing, but that she has understood me anyway, like some kind of mistranslation.

As she talks about her day, I find myself thinking about those empty wine glasses and the half-finished bottle of red left at the restaurant. I wonder whose fault it was. Whether it was him, his infidelities, his inadequacies, or whether it was her being overdramatic, making something out of nothing. I wonder why he is staying at the guesthouse. Maybe he is only visiting town, returning for business, or to tie up loose ends. Or perhaps he has been kicked out by the woman he was with. Clara is moaning about a fussy client at the hostel. I nod and agree how bad it must be. I don't really feel like speaking about the hostel any more, so decide to compliment her on the food to change the subject. She smiles and thanks me.

After we have cleared away the plates, I suggest going out to have a drink. She looks at me and smiles again. 'But why? There is plenty to drink here,' she says. 'Why don't we stay in?' She takes her glass into the front room and makes herself comfortable on the sofa.

I insist that we go out. When she realises that I am serious, her mood quickly changes and she seems to take offence at what I've said. I am very welcome to go and have a drink by myself, she tells me, but she would prefer to stay where she is. I thank her for the food, finish my beer and head out.

I walk as quickly as I can. It is late, but the bars are still full, with customers clutching *cañas* and spilling out into the streets. I reach the plaza where I sat before. The waiter is folding up unoccupied chairs. The young couple have disappeared. I stand in the plaza for a moment, wondering which way to go, before settling on the direction of the studio, to go home and sleep.

FORTY-ONE

THAT NIGHT SHE wants to eat out at a restaurant. I wear a shirt and let her choose where we eat. The restaurant's tables all have a mahogany finish. She looks at the menu for a very long time and, even when the waiter is standing over us, she can't decide. I order something or other. Finally she chooses the spaghetti Bolognese. It is the last thing on the menu I would choose. The waiter heads off. She asks me a question but my mind is elsewhere. I say, 'Have you ever been to Europe?'

She says no and, dismissing my question, asks me again what she'd originally said: something about going for a drink with her friends on Friday. I nod and say I think I am free. When her meal comes out, I become obsessed with watching her slowly twirl spaghetti around her fork. Every moment I can, I glance down at her plate. The sauce seems too orange, looks too sweet. It doesn't look Italian. She eats it very carefully, with no mess at all. I imagine eating with Stefani for a moment, at some restaurant in Bari. She too would eat tidily, I decide.

Laura talks about her day. I ask her how the Bolognese is. Fantastic, she tells me. I ask if it tastes authentic – as good as she's tasted, she tells me. I nod.

I manage to maintain our conversation throughout the meal. Afterwards, we head to the taxi rank. I feel a little light-headed from the wine. It is a clear night and, looking up to the sky, I can see more stars than normal. As we amble along, Laura tells me I am particularly quiet. I feel she is reproaching me for not talking to her. I say it's not her fault, it is only because I was looking up at the sky. She drops her accusing tone and loops her arm through mine, although I'm unsure if this is because she too has been taken in by the beauty of the sky, or because she is perplexed by my preoccupations.

At the taxi rank, she leans forward and kisses me gently. As she gets into her taxi, she smiles affectionately at me, before closing the door. I feel a little flutter of contentment and decide to walk home instead of taking a taxi.

FORTY-TWO

I'VE REALISED THAT in this heat, the heat of the late afternoon, even the birds keep out of the sun. A few people are now venturing out, probably to get back to the office after their lunch and a nap.

After a few days of living off my spare change, I go to the cashpoint. Finally I have some bills in my pocket. I still have no idea how much is left in my checking account, nor do I want to know.

The money in my pocket lightens my mood somewhat. It would be too much to say that it gives me freedom, but I feel I now have far more choice in what I do, and realise that I must have missed that in the days beforehand. I break a twenty buying a newspaper from a kiosk. It is indecipherable. Still, I fold it, tuck it under my arm and continue walking.

I take my spot on the wall. It takes me a moment to get comfortable. I unfold the newspaper and focus on the top paragraphs, letting my gaze cross the top of the pages, across the street, to the doorway. Nothing makes any sense.

I have no idea how long I spend sitting on the wall. One hour? Two hours? Three? I wriggle to keep comfortable. A lady who passed me earlier returns, coming from the opposite direction, this time with her child in tow. The child is scraping his feet, but his mother is ignoring this. I look at his scuffed, leather shoes. They must do this every day, I think.

His mother asks him something, but the child is reluctant to talk.

I look both ways down the street. Some pensioners are approaching from the distance. They seem to take an eternity to reach me and then another as they head off, away from me. I continue to focus on the open doorway.

I am certain I can make something out in the doorway. From the dimly lit passageway, a shadow has appeared, stretching out towards the street. Someone has come down into the lobby and is speaking to the guesthouse owner, I am sure. I cannot see who it is, nor the front desk, yet the shadow looks like it is nodding. It nods again. Something is being agreed. Is this someone paying up? Are they checking out?

The shadow stretches even further towards the street. I have the newspaper up so high that only the top of my gaze reaches over it. My heart is pounding like I never expected it to.

And at that moment a cab pulls up. The indicators are on, all flashing. Out of the guesthouse steps the moustached gentleman, clutching his caramel-coloured suitcase. He leans towards the open taxi window. I must have lowered my newspaper without realising, as I am staring at the taxi as hard as I can, staring at the moustached gentleman, trying to take everything in. I can no longer hear the people in the street, nor the traffic – only the hum of the taxi engine. He is going to get away, I know it.

'How could he . . .' I utter and, as soon as I have, I am shocked to hear what I have just whispered, shocked at my sense of injustice. I have not been treated unfairly – I have never been treated unfairly. I find myself where I am not through any ill-treatment, nor through any cursed luck; I have made the choices I've made, followed them through unencumbered, and yet . . . That image returns. That questioning look, shot across to me from this very gentleman, shot across the guesthouse reception, straight into me, no more than a moment to assess me, to know me, then return to his business. Mine no more than a fleeting appearance in an ever-revolving cast of passersby, a presence that, to him, was no more than a bit-part role in his theatre of plazas, arcades and boulevards. And just as his taxi door slams, just before the sound of the street returns – the sound of the passersby, of the traffic, of church bells ringing streets away, of the sparrows chirping as they hop along the wall beside me – I catch those words '. . . la estación . . .' directed at the taxi driver, but escaping momentarily into the street. I have dropped the newspaper. I suddenly find myself running, running as fast as I can. First ahead of the taxi, but the faster I push my legs, the more ground the taxi makes on me, until it is ahead, far ahead.

I see another taxi ahead of me, pulled over, waiting. I yank open the door. 'La estación,' I plead. The driver returns a blank look, as surprised as he is confused. 'La estación, la estación!' I am shouting. My hands are shaking. My palms are sweating again. He doesn't understand me. I can feel tears flooding towards my eyes.

'La estación . . .' I let out desperately. He turns and sets the meter. I am still unsure whether he has understood me. The taxi pulls out. It doesn't matter, I tell myself. We are moving, at least. We are going somewhere. I am breathless and sink into the back seat.

He has understood me. We pull into the train station. Already, my eyes are searching for the moustached man. The fare is eight euros. I give the driver ten and leap out of the cab. The entrance is too crowded for me to run, but I stride as quickly as I can through to the centre of the concourse. My eyes dart from person to person, then past their expressionless faces, seeking lines of sight to the distant platforms and far corners of the main hall.

I can feel my heart slowly sinking, my breath slowing. I walk along the station hall, glancing across at each platform. The tracks are either empty, or cleaners and ticket conductors are nipping in and out of carriages, with clear plastic bags full of paper coffee cups and drinks cans. The station is already emptying, a different place to the swarming hub it is earlier in the day. From across the station hall, I can hear baristas whacking portafilters against bins and releasing steam from espresso machines as they close shop. Some of the staff behind the ticket desks have also begun to leave, collecting their coats and saying their goodbyes.

FORTY-THREE

JOE CALLED ME on the house phone. He wanted to grab a drink with me, wanted to catch up. I still hadn't got round to replacing my cell. I began to wonder exactly how long he had been trying to get in touch. He hadn't heard from me and was dying to know about my trip to Europe, he insisted. Alyson split up with me, I replied. He said he knew.

A drink after work on Wednesday would work for him, he told me. There was a new wine bar on Washington Avenue that I should see. It sounded like the type of place that would make me feel uncomfortable, all low-lighting, couples and young professionals, but I couldn't think of anywhere better to go. We agreed to meet at 7pm.

Work actually went okay that Wednesday. Maybe I was looking forward to seeing Joe. In any case, I was a bit restless and didn't fancy heading home to talk to my parents – not just yet, anyway. At twenty past five I shut down my computer and took my coat. 'Have a nice evening,' I said to Robert. He smiled and then went straight back to his work. I looked across the office. Laura had already left. I headed for the door.

I walked quickly. Realising I was going to arrive well ahead of 7pm, I took a detour down Mills Street.

There were a few shops I hadn't seen before. I stopped briefly to look in each window. I didn't care much for the new clothes boutiques, but there was a small patisserie-café that caught my eye. I stopped and peered intently through the glass.

The window was full of decorated cakes and fresh baguettes, displayed on tiered wooden shelving. But past all this, something caught my eye. I moved closer to the window. Something shone. I fixed my gaze over the top of the layers of swirled, decorative icing. A small, golden earring glinted – glinted from the bottom of a slender earlobe. A fringe, swept behind the ear, that at its tip curled towards the chin.

A thick, styled bob.

Alyson's thick, styled bob,

Alyson's fringe,

Alyson's earlobe and

Alyson's small, golden earring.

Granville continued to peer through the patisserie-café window, over the tops of the decorated cakes. Peering at that shining, golden earring, itself pointed to by the swept fringe of that thick, styled bob, adorned by the girl whose brusque text message had sent his cellphone to the floor of the Mediterranean. And across from this girl sat another guy, confidently gesturing, recounting something to Alyson, making her smile, making her laugh. This other guy couldn't possibly be her date, he initially thought, couldn't possibly, but the more he stared, the more apparent this became.

And although Alyson sat away from her date, Granville noticed how she aligned her body directly at him, occasionally looking him deep in the eyes, cautious yet intense. The drama of the patisserie-café continued around them – customers going up to the till to collect coffees and pastries, the waitress frothing milk, staff clearing tables – the drama continued as if nothing were happening, as if this crime in front of Granville's eyes were not taking place. Alyson remained spellbound by this brute opposite her. This couldn't be, Granville told himself. His hair was too thickly gelled. His shirt was tucked in, too tucked in, if that were possible. From his spot on the sidewalk outside, Granville tried to make out their conversation. This guy's responses seemed short and blasé. He was sitting too confidently, as if in little doubt of his powers of seduction. His hand reached out to touch hers. And Granville, now trembling, could sense the goose pimples run up her arm, sense her body freeze, unable to react, craving to.

They continued to talk. He continued his series of abrupt responses. She should have been put off by his arrogance, yet the more aloof he became, the more she persisted with the conversation, just looking at him, rolling her bottom lip under her teeth.

Granville's eyes watered and, unable to take any more, he turned to run. And as Granville stumbled away, the guy with Alyson looked up out of the window and caught sight of him fleeing. An expression of confusion crossed the guy's face, before souring to something between disgust and pity. Yet Alyson, with her fringe swept towards her gleaming earring, never looked towards the window, never looked towards the fleeing Granville, and, instead, kept her eyes fixed on the brute in front of her.

FORTY-FOUR/FORTY-FIVE

I HAVE BEEN staring at the ceiling for so long I no longer know what time it is. All I want is sleep, yet it won't come. Easing myself off the bed, I pull on some jeans and a T-shirt, and lace up my Nikes. There's half a glass of wine on the desk. I put it to my nose, a waft of fetid acidity hitting my nostrils. Taking my keys, I leave the studio *and, leaving the house,* head into the street. As I close the front door behind me, a couple of birds take flight from the branch outside my bedroom window. It is the dead of night, but there is a soft, warm breeze and just enough moonlight to trace the outlines of the tree's branches.

I walk for five minutes without seeing a soul. Finally, a taxi rattles past with its toplight off, the driver heading home having finished his shift. I dig my hands into my pockets – not because of the cold, but through habit. I head for Tenney Park, *heading straight for the river,* to stand on the bridge, to lean over its edge. I keep my head down as I pass the moustached man's guesthouse, the vacancies sign still lit up, *past yesterday's patisserie-café, the shutters down, the lights off.* A tramp is asleep on a bench, the dregs of a quart of beer unfinished in the bottle beside him.

I reach the bridge. *Streetlamps line the river's path,* meaning you can just about make out the row of small jetties further down the bank. I lean over the railings, looking down at the water. I can only see its shimmer – no current, no flow – just dancing glints of light.

Closing my eyes, I think of Stefani, of that station cafe in Bari, then of her boathouse on the lake in Lombardy, of the jetty that stretches out over its own shimmering water. I push my leg through the railings, letting it hang it over the water, and imagine it dangling over that lake, the sun beating on the water's surface. The jetty creaks slightly; I can hear children shouting as they play in the water further round the water's edge. I imagine getting up from the jetty and beginning to walk around the lake. Birds are chirping; there is no one about. It will only be a short walk, to stretch my legs, to get some fresh air. Stefani would be back at the boathouse, waiting for me, engrossed in a novel by some Italian author I have never heard of. There would be something cold to drink in the fridge, for when I return. I snap out of this daydream and look back at my leg, dangling over the river, *dangling over the estuary*, dangling over the darkness.

I can no longer live like this, I tell myself, as decisively as I can. I can no longer bear it here, bear being here, being myself, this feeling of isolation, self-inflicted, I know, but unescapable, unchangeable. That impetus I had – and with it, that hope, that direction – faded long ago, no sooner, if I'm honest, than when I arrived back home, shrugged off my backpack and stood in the front yard, Dad's Honda on the drive in front of me, *no sooner, if I'm honest, than when I first set foot in Sevilla and walked out of the station, the heat visibly rippling from the sidewalks and roads.*

All that's left is to go back. Tomorrow, I'll buy a ticket, the first flight I can get on. A ticket in my hand, a token of impetus. Visas and bureaucracy could go fuck themselves: I have to go, at any cost.

My head is spinning. I leave the water's edge and begin to trudge back through the eerily quiet streets. I dig my hands deeper into my jeans pockets. Tomorrow I am leaving, I know it. Drop everything and head back. My heart is beating faster, yet settled on what I am about to do, I feel calmer.

I think back to being sat on that jetty in Triana, the sun on my neck, warming every fine hair along my collar. That decision to stay – *to go back* – for what? To sit passively observing the workings of Señora Rosales' small business? *The green folders and black biros of the office?* For those chance meetings with Clara, at the trellised bar serving *carrilladas? This self-destructive affliction – made up of both fear and longing – for a chance meeting with Alyson, a chance to tell her – to tell her what?* Those desperate attempts to pin some kind of grander meaning onto those lives that briefly passed through my own? *Those lunchtime coffees – away from the burrito place – those Friday night daiquiris and the queue at the taxi rank?* How naïve I had been, what an idiot I was.

I continue back towards the old town, *back into Madison*, head to that apartment from where I'd fled, fleeing to that plaza only to find the waiter clearing up cutlery and unfinished glasses of wine; *back towards to her parents' address, not knowing if she still lives there or has moved out, moved on, or moved in with some other.*

I stand at the end of the drive. All the lights are out. It briefly crosses my mind that leaving without saying a word would be the thing to do. She either has no idea I'm back, or most probably, does know, yet doesn't care.

I walk up the drive, but hesitate before pressing the buzzer. It's no time of night to be calling, but I'll never see her again. I cave immediately and begin ringing, ringing again and again.

Nobody answers. Nobody even stirs. I dig around in my pockets and find a scrap of paper. I write a note and slot it into the crack where the buzzer meets the wall, not even bothering to write her name.

You know I'm back. Or if you didn't, you do now. In any case, it never crossed your mind to call. So maybe it's not a question of knowing, but caring. I wanted to see you before I left. Explain myself a little. My mind's been anywhere but here. I'm heading back to that sky serene *and leaving these sun-baked streets* – things that should mean something, but with my mind so far from here, what can they? Just as long as you know it's not a question of not caring, but . . . Well, I'm not really sure.

    Granville

I try her buzzer one last time, before heading back in the direction of the studio.

And as I trudge back home, a light breeze ruffles my hair and cools my face, and I think of tomorrow, of the airline ticket in my hand, of heading back to the other side of the Atlantic. *Of having that ticket in my hand*, of looking at it and, again, finally, feeling I have some kind of direction.

ACKNOWLEDGEMENTS

ALTHOUGH MY FAMILY knew nothing of my writing until the publication of this novel, it is only because of their unconditional love and support that I have been able to pursue the choices I've made in life, and, through those, found my inspiration to write. Thank you most of all to my mother, Elizabeth, who, more than anyone, has understood and embraced my years abroad.

A thank-you to friends who read the early drafts, and, in particular, to Gloria Sanders, Marta Gebalska, Owen Parsons and Lucy Morel, whose feedback helped shape and refine them.

Thank you too to Rosa López Martínez and Juan Ramón Gallardo Pozas, who have presented me with unprecedented opportunity.

The biggest thank-you, though, goes to the team at Salt Publishing, and to my editor, Nicholas Royle. It is the dream of any budding writer to be published, but an absolute privilege to have your book edited by an author whose work you've admired.

NEW FICTION FROM SALT

RON BUTLIN
Billionaires' Banquet (978-1-78463-100-0)

NEIL CAMPBELL
Sky Hooks (978-1-78463-037-9)

SUE GEE
Trio (978-1-78463-061-4)

CHRISTINA JAMES
Rooted in Dishonour (978-1-78463-089-8)

V.H. LESLIE
Bodies of Water (978-1-78463-071-3)

WYL MENMUIR
The Many (978-1-78463-048-5)

ALISON MOORE
Death and the Seaside (978-1-78463-069-0)

ANNA STOTHARD
The Museum of Cathy (978-1-78463-082-9)

STEPHANIE VICTOIRE
The Other World, It Whispers (978-1-78463-085-0)

ALSO AVAILABLE FROM SALT

ELIZABETH BAINES
Too Many Magpies (978-1-84471-721-7)
The Birth Machine (978-1-907773-02-0)

LESLEY GLAISTER
Little Egypt (978-1-907773-72-3)

ALISON MOORE
The Lighthouse (978-1-907773-17-4)
The Pre-War House and Other Stories (978-1-907773-50-1)
He Wants (978-1-907773-81-5)
Death and the Seaside (978-1-78463-069-0)

ALICE THOMPSON
Justine (978-1-78463-031-7)
The Falconer (978-1-78463-009-6)
The Existential Detective (978-1-78463-011-9)
Burnt Island (978-1-907773-48-8)
The Book Collector (978-1-78463-043-0)

RECENT FICTION FROM SALT

KERRY HADLEY-PRYCE
The Black Country (978-1-78463-034-8)

CHRISTINA JAMES
The Crossing (978-1-78463-041-6)

IAN PARKINSON
The Beginning of the End (978-1-78463-026-3)

CHRISTOPHER PRENDERGAST
Septembers (978-1-907773-78-5)

MATTHEW PRITCHARD
Broken Arrow (978-1-78463-040-9)

JONATHAN TAYLOR
Melissa (978-1-78463-035-5)

GUY WARE
The Fat of Fed Beasts (978-1-78463-024-9)

NEW BOOKS FROM SALT

XAN BROOKS
The Clocks in This House All Tell Different Times
(978-1-78463-093-5)

RON BUTLIN
Billionaires' Banquet (978-1-78463-100-0)

MICKEY J C ORRIGAN
Project XX (978-1-78463-097-3)

MARIE GAMESON
The Giddy Career of Mr Gadd (deceased)
(978-1-78463-118-5)

LESLEY GLAISTER
The Squeeze (978-1-78463-116-1)

NAOMI HAMILL
How To Be a Kosovan Bride (978-1-78463-095-9)

CHRISTINA JAMES
Fair of Face (978-1-78463-108-6)